Murder, Secrets, Kisses, and Lies

EXCERPTS FROM THE KISS & THRILL AUTHORS

Carey Baldwin

Manda Collins

Lena Diaz

Rachel Grant

Krista Hall

Gwen Hernandez

CONTENTS

About Kiss and Thrill

Kiss and Thrill is a group blog devoted to romantic thrillers, mysteries, and suspense. To date, the nine Kiss and Thrill contributors have published twenty-seven books with ten publishers (including self-published titles), been nominated for the Golden Heart award nineteen times, and won twice. For more information on Sarah Andre, Carey Baldwin, Diana Belchase, Manda Collins, Lena Diaz, Rachel Grant, Krista Hall, Gwen Hernandez, or Sharon Wray, please visit our blog at www.KissandThrill.com.

WITNESS

IMPULSE

CONFESSION

CAREY BALDWIN

Award winning author, Carey Baldwin, brings you the story of a serial killer out for blood--and the only woman who can stop his reign of terror.

They say the Santa Fe Saint comes to save your soul--by taking your life.

Newly minted psychiatrist Faith Clancy gets the shock of her life when her first patient confesses to the grisly Saint murders. By law Faith's compelled to notify the authorities, but is her patient really the Saint? Or will she contribute to more death by turning the wrong man over to the police?

Faith is going to need all her wits and the help of a powerful adversary, Luke Jericho, if she's to unravel the truth. But she doesn't realize she's about to become an unwitting pawn in a serial killer's diabolical game. For once he's finished with Faith, she's to become his next victim.

CONFESSION
By Carey Baldwin

PROLOGUE

Saint Catherine's School for Boys
Near Santa Fe, New Mexico
Ten years ago—Friday, August 15, 11:00 p.m.

I'M NOT AFRAID of going to hell. Not one damn bit.

We're deep in the woods, miles from the boys' dormitory, and my thighs are burning because I walked all this way with Sister Bernadette on my back. Now I've got her laid out on the soggy ground underneath a hulking ponderosa pine. A bright rim of moonlight encircles her face. Black robes flow around her, engulfing her small body and blending with the night. Her face, floating on top of all that darkness, reminds me of a ghost head in a haunted house—but she's not dead.

Not yet.

My cheek stings where Sister scratched me. I wipe the spot

with my sleeve and sniff the air soaked with rotting moss, sickly-sweet pinesap, and fresh piss. I pissed myself when I clubbed her on the head with that croquet mallet. Ironic, since my pissing problem is why I picked Sister Bernadette in the first place. She ought to have left that alone.

I hear a gurgling noise.

Good.

Sister Bernadette is starting to come around.

This is what I've been waiting for.

With her rosary wound tightly around my forearm, the grooves of the carved sandalwood beads cutting deep into the flesh of my wrist, I squat on rubber legs, shove my hands under her armpits, and drag her into a sitting position against the fat tree trunk. Her head slumps forward, but I yank her by the hair until her face tilts up, and her cloudy eyes open to meet mine. Her lips are moving. Syllables form within the bubbles coming out of her mouth. I press my stinging cheek against her cold, sticky one.

Like a lover, she whispers in my ear, "God is merciful."

The nuns have got one fucked-up idea of mercy.

"Repent." She's gasping. "Heaven ..."

"I'm too far gone for heaven."

The God I know is just and fierce and is never going to let a creep like me through the pearly gates because I say a few Hail Marys. "God metes out justice, and that's how I know *I* will not be going to heaven."

To prove my point, I draw back, pull out my pocketknife, and press the silver blade against her throat. Tonight, I am more than a shadow. A shadow can't feel the weight of the knife in his palm. A shadow can't shiver in anticipation. A shadow is not to be feared, but I am not a shadow. Not in this moment.

She moves her lips some more, but this time, no sound comes out. I can see in her eyes what she wants to say to me. *Don't do it. You'll go to hell.*

I twist the knife so that the tip bites into the sweet hollow of her throat. "I'm not afraid of going to hell."

It's the idea of purgatory that makes my teeth hurt and my stomach cramp and my shit go to water. I mean, what if my heart isn't black enough to guarantee me a passage straight to hell? What if God slams down his gavel, and says, *Son, you're a sinner, but I have to take your family situation into account. That's a mitigating circumstance.*

A single drop of blood drips off my blade like a tear.

"What if God sends me to purgatory?" My words taste like puke on my tongue. "I'd rather dangle over a fiery pit for eternity than spend a single day of the afterlife in a place like this one."

I watch a spider crawl across her face.

My thoughts crawl around my brain like that spider.

You could make a pretty good case, I think, that St. Catherine's School for Boys is earth's version of purgatory. I mean, it's a place where you don't exist. A place where no one curses you, but no one loves you, either. Sure, back home, your father hits you and calls you a bastard, but you *are* a bastard, so it's okay he calls you one. Behind me, I hear the sound of rustling leaves and cast a glance over my shoulder.

Do it! You want to get into hell, don't you?

I turn back to Sister and flick the spider off her cheek.

The spider disappears, but I'm still here.

At St. Catherine's, no one notices you enough to knock you around. Every day is the same as the one that came before it, and the one that's coming after. At St. Catherine's, you wait and wait for your turn to leave, only guess what, you dumb-ass bastard, your turn is *never* going to come, because you, my friend, are in purgatory, and you can't get out until you repent.

Sister Bernadette lets out another gurgle.

I spit right in her face.

I won't repent, and I can't bear to spend eternity in purgatory, which is I why I came up with a plan. A plan that'll rocket me straight past purgatory, directly to hell.

Sister Bernadette is the first page of my blueprint. I have the book to guide me the rest of the way. For her sake, not mine, I make the sign of the cross.

She's not moving, but her eyes are open, and I hear her breathing. I want her to know she is going to die. "You are going to help me get into hell. In return, I will help you get into heaven."

I shake my arm and loosen the rosary. The strand slithers down my wrist. One bead after another drops into my open palm, electrifying my skin at the point of contact. My blood zings through me, like a high-voltage current. I am not a shadow.

A branch snaps, making my hands shake with the need to hurry.

What are you waiting for, my friend?

Is Sister Bernadette afraid?

She has to be. Hungry for her fear, I squeeze my thighs

together, then I push my face close and look deep in her eyes.

"The blood of the lamb will wash away your sins." She gasps, and her eyes roll back. "Repent."

My heart slams shut.

I begin the prayers.

Chapter One

Santa Fe, New Mexico
Present Day—Saturday, July 20, 1:00 p.m.

MAN, SHE'S SOMETHING.

Luke Jericho halted midstride, and the sophisticated chatter around him dimmed to an indistinct buzz. Customers jamming the art gallery had turned the air hot, and the aromas of perfume and perspiration clashed. His gaze sketched the cut muscles of the woman's shoulders before swerving to the tantalizing V of her low-back dress. There, slick fabric met soft skin just in time to hide the thong she must be wearing. His fingers found the cold silk knot of his tie and worked it loose. He let his glance dot down the line of her spine, then swoop over the arc of her ass. It was the shimmer of Mediterranean blue satin, illuminated beneath art lights, that had first drawn his eye, her seductive shape that had pulled him up short, but it was her stance—her pose—that had his blood expanding like hot mercury under glass.

Head tilted, front foot cocked back on its stiletto, the woman studied one of Luke's favorite pieces—his brother Dante's mixed-media. A piece Luke had hand-selected and quietly inserted into this show of local artists in the hopes a positive response might bolster his brother's beleaguered self-esteem.

The woman couldn't take her eyes off the piece, and he couldn't take his eyes off the woman. Her right arm floated, as if she were battling the urge to reach out and touch the multitextured painting. Though her back was to him, he could picture her face, pensive, enraptured. Her lips would be parted and sensual. He savored the swell of her bottom beneath the blue dress. Given the way the fabric clung to her curves, he'd obviously guessed right about the thong. She smoothed the satin with her hand, and he rubbed the back of his neck with his palm. *Ha.* Any minute now, she'd turn and ruin his fantasy with what was sure to turn out to be the most ordinary mug in the room.

And then she did turn, and damned if her mug wasn't ordinary at all, but she didn't appear enraptured. Inquisitive eyes, with a distinct undercurrent of melancholy, searched the room and found him. Then, delicate brows raised high, her mouth firmed into a hard line—even thinned, her bloodred lips were temptation itself—she jerked to a rigid posture and marched, yeah, marched, straight at him.

Hot ass. Great mouth. Damn lot of nerve.

"I could feel your stare," she said.

"Kind of full of yourself, honey."

A flush of scarlet flared across her chest, leading his attention to her lovely, natural breasts, mostly, but not entirely, concealed by a classic neckline. With effort, he raised his eyes to meet hers. Green. Skin, porcelain. Hair, fiery—like her cheeks—and flowing. She looked like a mermaid. Not the soft kind, the kind with teeth.

"I don't like to be ogled." Apparently, she intended to stand her ground.

He decided to stand his as well. That low-back number she had on might be considered relatively tame in a room with more breasts on display than a Picasso exhibit, but there was something about *the way she wore it.* "Then you shouldn't have worn that dress, darlin'."

Her brow arched higher in challenge. "Which is it? Honey or darlin'?"

"Let's go with honey. You look sweet." Not at the moment she didn't, but he'd sure like to try to draw the sugar out of her.

This woman was easily as interesting and no less beautiful than his best gallery piece, and she didn't seem to be reacting to him per the usual script. He noticed his hand floating up, reaching out, just as her hand had reached for the painting. Like his mesmerizing customer, he knew better than to touch the display, but it was hard to resist the urge.

Her body drew back, and her shoulders hunched. "You're aware there's a serial killer on the loose?"

Luke, you incredible ass.

No wonder she didn't appreciate his lingering looks. Every woman he knew was on full alert. The Jericho charm might or might not be able to get him out of this one, but he figured she was worth a shot. "Here, in this gallery? In broad daylight?" He searched the room with his gaze and made his tone light. "Or are you saying you don't like being sized up for the kill?" He patted his suit pockets, made a big show of it, then stroked his chin thoughtfully. "I seem to have misplaced my rosary somewhere; I don't suppose you've seen it?"

Her shoulders eased back to a natural position.

"Seriously, do I look like someone who'd be called *the Saint*?"

If the glove doesn't fit …

Her lips threatened to curve up at the corners. "No. I don't suppose you do." Another beat, then her smile bloomed in earnest. "Looking a little is one thing, maybe it's even flattering … but you seem to have exceeded your credit line."

He turned his palms up. "Then I'd like to apply for an increase."

At that, her pretty head tipped back, and she laughed, a big genuine laugh. It was the kind of laugh that was a touch too hearty for a polished society girl, which perhaps she wasn't after all. It was also the kind of laugh he'd like to hear again. Of its own accord, his hand found his heart. "Listen, I'm honest-to-God sorry if I spooked you. That wasn't my intention."

Her expression was all softness now.

"Do you like the painting?" he asked, realizing that he cared more than he should about the answer.

"It's quite … dark." Her bottom lip shivered with the last word, and he could sense she found Dante's painting disturbing.

Always on the defensive where his brother was concerned, his back stiffened. He tugged at his already loosened tie. "Artists are like that. I don't judge them."

"Of course. I-I wasn't judging the artist. I was merely making an observation about the painting. It's expressive, beautiful."

Relaxing his stance, he pushed a hand through his hair.

She pushed a hand through her hair, then her glance found her fancy-toed shoes. "Maybe I overreacted, maybe you weren't even staring."

Giving in to the urge to touch, he reached out and tilted her chin up until their eyes met. "I'm Luke Jericho, and you had it right the first time. I *was* staring. I was staring at—" He barely had time to register a startled flash of her green eyes before she turned on her heel and disappeared into the throng of gallery patrons.

He shrugged and said to the space where her scent still sweetened the air, "I was staring at your fascination. Your fascination fascinates me.

CAREY BALDWIN IS a mild-mannered doctor by day and an award winning, bestselling author of edgy suspense by night. She holds two doctoral degrees, one in medicine and one in psychology. She loves reading and writing stories that keep you off balance and on the edge of your seat. Carey lives in the southwestern United States with her amazing family. In her spare time she enjoys hiking and chasing wildflowers. Carey loves to hear from readers so please visit her at www.CareyBaldwin.com, on Facebook www.facebook.com/CareyBaldwinAuthor, or Twitter @CareyBaldwin.

BOOKS BY CAREY BALDWIN

Confession (March 2014)

Judgment: A Cassidy & Spenser Thriller (Oct 2014)

Vengeance: A Cassidy & Spenser Thriller (Spring 2015)

Redemption: A Cassidy & Spenser Thriller (Fall 2015)

First Do No Evil (June 2012)

Hush (June 2013)

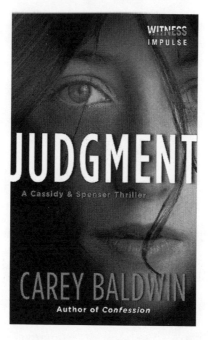

Judgment: A Cassidy & Spenser Thriller (Oct 2014)

Carey Baldwin, author of the bestselling novel, *Confession*, returns with a new series featuring two of her most beloved characters. Fans of dark psychological suspense will devour this riveting story of rivals caught in a killer's twisted web.

When a coed falls prey to a sadistic killer, forensic psychiatrist Dr. Caitlin Cassidy and Special Agent Atticus Spenser are called in to testify—one for the defense, one for the prosecution. With warring approaches on justice, these two rivals have been butting heads for years—both in the courtroom and out. And at first, this case appears to be no different.

But when a brutal attack leaves the accused man dead and Caity in critical condition, petty differences take a backseat to saving lives. As the lone survivor, Caity knows too much and the killer—a madman calling himself the Man in the Maze—is coming back for round two. Now, Caity and Spense must join forces to uncover the killer's identity before Caity's time—and luck—runs out.

*One
lovely lady
knows...*

WHY LORDS LOSE THEIR HEARTS

MANDA COLLINS

Author of *Why Earls Fall in Love*

THE TRUTH COULD RUIN HER

In Manda Collins's *Why Lords Lose Their Hearts*, Perdita, the widowed Duchess of Ormonde, keeps a dangerous secret—the truth of how her brutish husband died. But a mysterious avenger seems to know it, too, and when anonymous threats turn into public attacks, there's only one friend she can turn to for help—her husband's former secretary, Lord Archer Lisle. The man who witnessed her every heartache. The kind of man whose love she can only dream of ...

WILL HIS LOVE SAVE HER?

The youngest of the Duke of Pemberton's five sons, Lord Archer Lisle is used to waiting his turn. For years, he could only stand by, seething, as Perdita suffered at the hands of her husband, but now she's under threat from another source—one who will stop at nothing to make her pay for the late duke's death. But the good-natured Archer can be dangerous when crossed—and he'll do anything to keep the woman he's adored for so long safe in his arms...

WHY LORDS LOSE THEIR HEARTS
BY MANDA COLLINS

PROLOGUE

"PUT THE KNIFE down, your grace," Perdita heard her friend, Mrs. Georgina Mowbray, say to Gervase as he held the pen-knife closer to her throat.

She wasn't sure how long they'd stood thus, her husband's sour breath panting across her cheek as he held her in a death grip against his powerful body. A while, at least. Time seemed to get away from her when Gervase was in one of his moods. And Perdita had found long ago that ignoring such things would make it easier to pretend later that it had never happened.

Only this time, she wasn't sure she'd need to pretend. If he killed her, she'd forget everything. Which for one blissful moment sounded as close to heaven as she'd ever come.

She'd known for a good while that things would come to this point. Gervase's moods had risen and fallen with much greater speed than they had when she'd first married him five years before. Then he'd seemed—in retrospect—almost normal. And she thought she was the luckiest woman in the world. But like everything else in life, there was a before and an after. A point at which one was able to judge things had changed irrevocably. For Perdita, it had been the first time he hit her. And everything after that had been hastily reshuffled into the 'after' pile.

If she hadn't had the courage to confess her predicament to her sister and their friend Georgie, who had both endured their own bruises at the hands of abusive husbands, she would still be in constant reaction mode. Never making things happen herself, but only responding to what others did. And, as Gervase's wife, that meant that she reacted to each blow, every threat, every insinuation that he held all the power while she held none.

Now, however, she'd learned to stand up to him. And finally, she and her sister and friend had judged it to be time for her to leave him. Perdita had known the discussion would not be an easy one, of course. She'd known he would lash out or worse, try to keep her from leaving. But even after years of his abuse she was still capable of being surprised. Which is what happened when he pulled the knife out and held it to her throat.

"Killing your wife will not make you feel any better." Georgie's voice was calmer than Perdita's would have been had their situations been reversed. But then Georgie had grown up following the drum, so was used to sounding authoritative.

They'd only wanted this to be the first step, Perdita reflected as his arms tightened around her. She would leave Ormond House and set up her own establishment. Since Gervase spent much of his time away anyway, it shouldn't be too taxing for him. It wasn't as if Perdita would be in the Antipodes. If he needed her, she'd be in Mayfair a few streets over.

But, they'd miscalculated. Not only had Gervase been unhappy about the plan, he translated his unhappiness into physical retribution against his wife. Which concluded in his pressing the blade of a knife to the vulnerable skin of her neck. He was not going to let her go without a fight.

His next words only confirmed it. "She wouldn't be able to leave me," the duke slurred. His lips twisted with resentment. "She was fine before the two of you got hold of her with your lies about me."

Afraid that he would turn his anger on her sister and friend, Perdita glanced over to see them exchanging a speaking look. To save them from being harmed by him, she considered telling him the truth, that she had chosen to make this appeal based on her own initiative. After so many years of enduring Ormond's cruelties, this week, Perdita had reached the point at which she no longer cared what her husband would do to retaliate against her for leaving. She only knew, she'd told her sister and Georgie, that if she did not leave now, she was unlikely to live for much longer.

If this was how Ormonde behaved when he suspected Perdita's friends of luring her away, though, his response to learning it had been Perdita's own idea would send him over the edge.

Deciding that she had to appease him somehow, Perdita said, "I would never leave you, darling." Trying desperately to remain calm even as she felt the press of his blade against her skin, she continued, "You know I love you."

While she waited for him to reply—the alcohol had made him a bit slow today—she dared a look at Isabella and Georgina again. This time she saw Georgie silently make a figure with her thumb and forefinger. To anyone who knew her and her penchant for carrying a small pistol in her reticule for safety, it was obvious. Perdita felt her heart speed up as Isabella gave a quick nod to let Georgie know she understood.

Perdita and Isabella had been slightly appalled when Georgina first informed them of her habit of carrying the small pistol in her reticule, but Georgie explained that she'd done so for her own protection in the peninsula, and it had simply become habit. And the two other women had reluctantly agreed that there were some occasions when having a pistol might be beneficial for a lady traveling alone in London.

Perdita was unsure whether she felt relief at knowing her friend was armed, or terrified that somehow Gervase would learn of it and punish her friend for it. Or worse, use it on all three of them. Georgie had often accused her of being too pessimistic, but in this case, she knew whereof she spoke. No one knew her husband's capacity for violence better than Perdita. And the Gervase she knew would not hesitate to shoot them if he decided it was what he wished.

Perhaps to distract him from Georgie and her pistol, Isabella began to speak. "Ormonde," she heard her sister say with the self-assurance that only Isabella could muster, then, perhaps thinking better of it, she softened her tone. "Gervase," Isabella said, switching to the duke's Christian name, "we aren't here to take Perdita away from you. We simply wish for you to perhaps be a bit gentler with her."

Perdita felt his arms tighten around her. "Why?" he demanded petulantly. "She's not gentle with me. She scratched my face earlier. Damn her." He shook her as he said those last words, and Perdita heard herself whimper.

Wondering if there was any possible way for her to get the knife out of his hand, Perdita's mind raced.

Isabella spoke up, again, her tone imperious now as she spoke to her brother in law. "You should be gentle with her because she might be carrying the next Duke of Ormonde." Perdita bit back a gasp at the suggestion. She wasn't enceinte, but he had no way of knowing that. And if it infused his heart with kindness and joy, so be it.

Unfortunately, their words only served to make him angrier. With a sound like a bull about to charge, he twisted Perdita's arm up behind her back.

Moving as one, Georgina and Isabella stepped forward. Closing her eyes, Perdita sent up a swift prayer that they'd survive.

"There, now," Isabella said, her voice placating, as if she were trying to soothe a skittish horse, "you don't wish to harm your heir, do you?"

But they'd no sooner stepped forward when it became clear Isabella's words had been woefully miscalculated. Rather than being transported with joy, Ormonde instead became even angrier. "What? Is this true?" he asked, turning Perdita in his arms so that he could look her in the face. She tried with some difficulty not to cringe back from him. "You lied to me?" he demanded. In his haste to get his hands on her, he brought the knife down where it became trapped between Perdita's arm and his own fist as he began to shake her. "You lying bitch! You told me it wasn't possible!" he cried.

"No!" Isabella shouted, rushing forward to pull him away from her sister. "Stop it! Stop it!"

"Your grace," Georgina said in a hard voice, stepping forward as she jerked the pistol upwards. "I warn you to stop that at once."

In a blur, Perdita watched Isabella grasp the duke by the shoulders and attempt to forcibly pry him away from her. When her sister finally managed to hook her arm around his neck, cutting off his airway, the duke gave a muffled growl and shoved his body backward as if trying to dislodge his attacker.

Finally as they spun away from her, Perdita saw Georgie lift her pistol, take aim and fire.

At almost the same time, the knife, which had been held between Perdita's body and Ormond's hand, fell to the floor, and must have been in the right position at the right time, because when the duke fell mere seconds later it was upon the same blade with which he'd threatened his wife.

Sliding to the floor in a heap, Perdita wept. Though she wasn't sure why.

CHAPTER ONE

"A PAIR OF PRIME goers, Lord Archer. The best I've ever seen at Tattersall's."

Lord Archer Lisle nodded and tried to look somewhat interested as the overeager Earl of Wrotham waxed rhapsodic over his new pair of matched bays. He was as fond of horseflesh as the next man, but tonight his mind was on another sort of flesh altogether.

He'd accepted the invitation to Lady Sumrall's annual ball knowing that Perdita, Duchess of Ormond would also be in attendance. In fact, Perdita's presence was the sole reason he'd chosen to come at all. Since both her sister, the former Lady Isabella Wharton now Duchess of Ormond, and her friend, the Countess of Coniston, had had their lives threatened by an as yet unknown assailant earlier in the year, the widowed duchess had become the sole focus of architect of their attacks. So far the threats had come in the form of anonymous notes taunting the widowed duchess with the knowledge that he—Archer assumed this person was a he—knew what she'd done last season, when her deceased husband, the brutish sixth Duke of Ormond, had been killed. Nevermind that the dead nobleman had been killed while attempting to cut his wife's throat. Whoever this mastermind was, he'd appointed himself judge and jury and had found all three women guilty of the crime of killing Ormond. Nevermind that there had been no suspicions, as far as Archer knew, from the authorities.

Thus far, the threats against her had not persuaded the headstrong Perdita to curb one of her normal activities, a resistance of which she was inordinately proud. But Archer, who had been there for the aftermath of the attempts on the lives of both the Duchess of Ormond and Lady Coniston, was not so happy about her resistance to any kind of curtailment of her behavior. Yes, he wished to see the coward who threatened her thwarted, and Perdita going about as if nothing was amiss did so, but knowing that her defiance put her life in jeopardy frightened him and he wasn't afraid to admit it. And since Perdita refused to listen to reason—especially when it came from the mouth of Lord Archer Lisle—he'd decided to see to it that she remained safe whether she chose to listen to him or not.

At present Perdita was waltzing with Lord Dunthorp, a viscount of middling years who had spent the last few weeks dancing attendance on her. Her luxuriant strawberry blond hair was dressed in a simple chignon that put the fussier styles of the other ladies to shame. And her gown, a cerise colored silk that was simply cut but hugged her slim figure in all the right places, also put the others to shame. He'd seen Dunthorp's eyes wander from her pretty face down to her impressive décolletage more than once since they'd taken to the floor—a circumstance that made Archer long to gut the other man, though it would be dashed bad manners to his hosts.

He'd been half in love with her ever since they'd met. And it hadn't taken long for that half to expand into a whole.

It wasn't just because she was beautiful—though she was. No, though he appreciated her fine-boned loveliness, it was her spirit that solidified his affection for her. Perdita wasn't an angel. What woman was? But she had a way about her. A sweetness in the way she dealt with people—he'd heard the servants at Ormond House speak of it—that set them at ease. Even her bad moods—which were rare—were short-lived and often ended with a self-deprecating remark.

But the thing that most endeared her to Archer was something she likely didn't even recall. It had been a moment some three years earlier when one of the housemaids had fallen pregnant. There were few secrets in a household as large as Ormond House, and Archer had a strong suspicion that it had been the duke or one of his cronies who forced himself upon the girl. But when the housekeeper had informed Perdita, she'd handled the matter with kindness and compassion, giving the maid enough money to return home to the country and with the offer of a reference should she need one in the future. Perdita hadn't considered the matter in terms of it's reflection on herself. She'd only considered the little maid's feelings. And it had been that bit of selflessness that did him in. From that moment on he'd been a goner. And in spite of himself he'd fallen all the way in love with his employer's wife.

From the corner of his eye, he could see her deep blue gown as they made the circuit of the Sumrall ballroom. He wasn't jealous. How could he be when his position as private secretary to the Duke of Ormond made her his virtual employer? And it wasn't as if the late duke's death had cleared the way for him. While Perdita was a duchess, Archer was still the younger son of a Duke with a courtesy title and only the expectation of a modest inheritance from a distant aunt. No, Perdita was not for the likes of him. No matter how he might, in his heart of hearts, wish to declare himself to her.

"I say, Lord Archer," Wrotham interrupted his thoughts. "I think Mrs. Fitzroy is attempting to get your attention."

Pulling himself together, Archer glanced across the room to see that indeed the comely widow was casting a speaking glance his way. And if he were any interpreter of glances, hers was saying something that was not appropriate in mixed company. The lady had been trying to lure him into her bed for weeks now, but though Archer could appreciate the joys of the bedchamber as much as the next man, he was too busy protecting Perdita from herself to succumb. Then there was the whole unrequited business.

He snagged a glass of champagne from a passing footman and took a drink before he spoke. "I believe you're correct Wrotham," he said nodding to the other man. "But I'm afraid I have other plans this evening. Lovely though Mrs. Fitzroy may be."

The other man touched his index finger to the side of his nose. "Say no more, old fellow," he said with a knowing look. "Just between us, I've heard Mrs. Fitzroy is a bit possessive, so it's probably just as well that you not try to juggle her with another woman, if you catch my meaning."

Since it was impossible not to catch Wrotham's meaning, Archer just nodded.

"I hope you won't mind if I have a bit of a try at her," the other man continued, straightening his cuffs as he placed his own empty champagne glass on an obliging side table. "It's just that I'm in search of a new mistress and I like the look of your Mrs. Fitzroy."

Archer would have told the other man to be his guest, but that would have implied that he did indeed have some sort of connection with her, so he simply nodded again and the two men parted ways.

The waltz having just ended, Archer threaded his way toward the side of the ballroom where Dunthorp had just left Perdita—presumably in search of champagne for her. But before he'd made it halfway there, their hostess clapped her hands from a position near where the musicians were set up. "Lords and ladies," she said once the chatter in the ballroom had descended to a low murmur, "if I could have your attention, please!"

Not wishing to do her the discourtesy of walking while she spoke, Archer paused.

"I am delighted to tell you that I've arranged a wonderful bit of theatre for you this evening, thanks to the gracious proprietors of the Theatre Royale," Lady Sumrall said. "For your enjoyment, we have not just one, but three superb actresses: leading lady of the stage, Mrs. Alicia Lloyd, her charming understudy Mrs. Pfeiffer and the soon to be famous ingénue, Miss Desdemona Wright. And playing opposite all three is the incomparable Mr. Charles Keating. All starring in a pantomime that is sure to bring everyone to rapturous applause!" As she introduced each of the actors, they stepped forward. Archer could see more than one gentleman eyeing the actresses, and Lord Carston, who was rumored to be Mrs. Lloyd's current paramour, beamed, despite the fact that his wife was also present in the room.

"Let the play, entitled 'The Secret' begin," Lady Sumrall said before stepping aside while the actors took their places before the —musicians' dais.

Intrigued despite himself, Archer folded his arms across his chest as the performance got underway.

Mrs. Pfeiffer and Miss Wright stood to one side while Mrs. Lloyd and Mr. Keating took center stage. Neither of them speaking, Mrs. Lloyd stood before an imaginary table arranging flowers, moving them this way and that as she assessed them. Behind her, Keating stormed forward, his face thunderous as he roughly touched her on the shoulder. As she turned in surprise, he brandished an invisible letter as if to admonish her with whatever was written there. Her eyes wide, Mrs. Lloyd clasped her hands before her, pleading with him as he glared at her, his grip on her arm tight and painful-looking. The actress exaggerated her actions, throwing her head and making as if to escape his grip. Then Keating gipped her by the shoulders and shook her.

Though it was obvious that the two were acting, Archer shifted his weight from one foot to the other, the scene making him uncomfortable.

From stage left, Mrs. Pfeiffer entered, and stomped her foot. Keating and Lloyd turned feigned shock. From stage right, Miss Wright entered and gasped loudly. Seeing the other woman, Keating pulled Mrs. Lloyd against him an invisible knife to her throat. Archer watched in dawning horror as Mrs. Pfeiffer clasped an invisible pistol between her hands and pulled the trigger. At the same time, Mrs. Lloyd twisted out of his grasp. Then Miss Wright and Mrs. Pfeiffer rushed toward Keating as he fell senseless to the floor. All three women embraced and stilled, the performance over as the ballroom erupted in thunderous applause.

His mouth agape, Archer stood motionless as the three actors took their bows and Lady Sumrall's guests continued to rain praise upon them. Then, he pushed his way through the crowd, desperate to get to where he'd last seen Perdita. Because he knew without doubt that she would have been as disturbed as he was by the performance.

Not because the subject matter was so shocking. One can and did see more melodrama at the theatre every evening of the week.

No, she'd be shocked by this show for another reason altogether.

Because the actors from the Theatre Royale hadn't simply been performing a play written for the entertainment of Lady Sumrall's guests. It had been written to instill fear in the heart of one person and one alone. Perdita.

The scene hadn't depicted a scene from the imagination of the playwright. It had been the retelling of a scene that was all too familiar to the widowed duchess. Because she'd not only witnessed it, but lived it.

On the day her husband died.

* * *

PERDITA, DUCHESS OF Ormond, stood chatting with Lady

Entwhistle on the side of the Sumrall ballroom, slightly out of breath from her waltz with Lord Dunthorp. He'd gone in search of champagne for them both, and if she were completely honest with herself, Perdita was slightly relieved to be out from beneath his watchful eye.

Dunthorp was a nice enough man, but his unrelenting pursuit of her had become a bit of a discomfort to her in the past few weeks. It wasn't that she disliked him. If that were so she'd have sent the man packing when he'd first begun to show interest. No, it was just that Perdita, having only last year emerged from beneath her husband's controlling thumb, was not quite ready to call someone else her lord and master. She liked being able to make her own decisions and come and go as she pleased. She enjoyed choosing her own gowns and not having to worry that the bruises he'd left on her the night before would show no matter how she tugged down the sleeves.

One would think that since her severed engagement to Lord Coniston she'd have learned her lesson about attaching herself to single gentlemen before she was quite sure of her feelings for them. Fortunately for her, her friend Georgina had married Coniston shortly thereafter, so he was none the worse for wear. Not that he would have been at any rate, since theirs had been a betrothal of convenience more than anything else. But Dunthorp was not as indifferent as Coniston had been, and Perdita had no more friends waiting in the wings to sweep him off his feet. And if her intuition was right, he was working up to offer for her sometime in the next few weeks. An offer she had no intention of accepting. And rejection would put an end to their friendship.

"Are you aware that Lord Archer Lisle is staring at you as if he wished to carry you off and ravish you, darling?" Lady Entwhistle asked, jerking Perdita from her reverie. "If I had a man of his looks desperate for me," she went on, "I'd not be wasting time here in Lady Sumrall's crowded ball room, darling, that's for sure."

"Don't be absurd, Letitia," Perdita said with a laugh, "Lord Archer is simply playing the duenna. He has taken it upon himself to look after me and he's worse than an old mother hen." That she found Lord Archer, with his golden good looks and tall, impressively strong physique, to be devilishly handsome was neither here nor there. She and Archer were friends. That was all, and as she'd just been telling herself she had no wish for another husband.

"If you say so, my dear Duchess," Lady Entwhistle, who was known for her affairs as much as she was for her impeccable taste, said with a shake of her head. "It's a shame, though, if you don't take advantage of all that deliciousness while you still can. Dunthorp is a nice enough man, but look at Lord Archer's shoulders!"

Perdita was saved from replying by their hostess who announced a particular entertainment had been arranged for them this evening. It had been thus since the beginning of the season. Each hostess of the ton had made it her business to outdo the ones preceding her. Thus, Lady Glenlivet had imported a real Venetian gondola to give rides in the pond behind her house in Hampstead, though that had come to grief when Lord Glenlivet had attempted to get a bit too close to his mistress in the boat and overturned it and them in the waist high water. Then Lady Moulton had hired a pair of acrobats from Astley's to perform in the garden of her Grosvenor Square townhouse, complete with flaming hoops through which they leapt most impressively...until one of the hoops caught a lemon tree aflame and the fire brigade had to be summoned. Now, it would seem, Lady Sumrall had found yet another means to entertain her guests. Though having mere actors perform in her ballroom was a bit of a letdown, if Perdita were to be honest with herself.

When the players had finished their little tableau, however, Perdita was gasping for breath and trying desperately to make her way through the crowded ballroom to one—any—of the doors leading into the rest of the house. She was on the point of shouting to make herself heard above the din of applause when she felt a strong arm guiding her.

"Easy," she heard Archer say before she could wrest herself from his hold. "I'll get you out of here," he told her, the reverberation of his voice at her ear strangely reassuring.

Silently, they pushed their way past what for Perdita was a blur of colorful gowns, black coats and white cravats toward the French doors at the back of the Sumrall ballroom. As soon as they stepped outside she was able to breathe again, and she gripped his arm tighter than was strictly necessary as he led her toward a picturesque little bower just out of range of the torchlight coming from the terrace.

"Sit," he said brusquely, and she knew that if she were in a different mood she'd have chided him for talking to her as if she were one of his spaniels. But she was so relieved to be out of the ballroom, she lowered herself to the little bench beneath the rose arbor and hugged her arms. It was then that she realized her teeth were chattering and with a curse, he sat down beside her and pulled against him, warming her with the heat from his body.

"I'd give you my coat but I don't think I can get the damned thing off with help," he muttered, rubbing her bare arms with his gloved hands. To her astonishment, she began to cry, with gulping, hideous little sobs that even as she heard them mortified her. But she was unable to stop herself, and Archer, being Archer, seemed prepared for it, and pulled her against his chest and let her sob into his beautifully tied cravat before giving her his handkerchief and instructing her to blow her nose.

When she had recovered herself and dried her eyes, Perdita pulled herself from the comfort of his arms and moved cautiously over a bit so that they were no longer plastered against one another like peas in a pod.

"I'm sorry for that," she said stiffly. "I don't know what came over me."

He laughed bitterly. "I'd say you were overset by seeing the scene of Gervase's death re-enacted before a ballroom full of London society," he said. "And I can't say I blame you."

She closed her eyes, the tableau blending with the actual scene in her mind as the horror of what had just happened revealed itself to her once more. Whoever it was that had been threatening her, had threatened Isabella and Georgina, was sending her a message. A very public and very terrifying message.

"He's raising the stakes," she said grimly. "He's no longer content to threaten me in private. He's willing to bring his threats out into the open. To risk my reputation by accusing me in a ballroom full of witnesses."

"But he's too much of a dam...dashed coward to reveal his own identity," Archer agreed. "Do you think anyone noticed your reaction to the pantomime?" he asked, his jaw tight.

Perdita thought back to the scene around her as the players had acted out their drama. But all she could remember was her own response to the show. The sick feeling in her stomach, and the dawning horror as she realized just what it was they were performing. Aloud she said, "I don't know. I was too intent upon my own reaction."

He nodded, and Perdita watched his profile as he stared out at the garden beyond them. They were silent for a few minutes, both lost in their own thoughts. Perdita wondered what would happen if someone had noticed her fleeing the ballroom with Archer at her side. Belatedly she remembered Lord Dunthorp and suspected that she might not need to worry about giving him the brush off now. Though she didn't want to marry him, she did feel bad for disappointing him. He was a nice man, and deserved better than that.

"You're going to have to leave town," Archer said, turning to her, his expression determined in the torchlight. "It's the only way you're going to keep this madman from ruining your reputation before the ton."

She stiffened. She'd lived with the fear that this person's threats had induced in her for months now. And though tonight's had been his most public attack upon her to date, she wasn't about to let him scare her from leaving the field altogether. "I disagree," she said firmly. "We don't even know if the others in the ballroom were even aware of the meaning of that little show. Why on earth should I allow him to make me leave town and let him think his threats are working?"

"They are working," he said hotly. "You were shaking a few minutes ago, and weeping. Or don't you remember that?"

She sat up straighter. "I don't like your tone, Lord Archer," Perdita said calmly.

"Well," he said, standing up to loom over her, "I don't like the way you're ignoring the very real danger this person poses." He ran a hand through his hair, leaving it sticking up on one side. "Perdita, he's already sent proxies to make attempts on both Isabella's and Georgina's lives. Everything he's done thus far has indicated that he means to make you pay the most for what happened to Gervase. Do you honestly wish to remain here while he escalates his campaign against you?"

"I am more than aware of what this person did, or tried to do to my sister and my friend," she retorted. "But that doesn't mean that I will simply walk away. Besides, how long should I remain in hiding? One year, two, ten? I'm not going to let someone with a vendetta against me dictate the terms of my life to me. If I do that he wins."

"But you'd be safe," he argued. "And Ormonde and Coniston and I could find him while you're away. When the coast is clear you could return."

She shook her head. "You don't understand. I spent years letting Gervase dictate my every move. I refuse to let someone I don't even know do the same. I'm sorry, Archer, but I can't do it. I won't."

He stared at her. She watched as it dawned on him that nothing he could say would change her mind. His lips tight, he said, "Then it would appear there's nothing left to be said." With a short bow, he left her.

He couldn't have gone very far before she heard him say, "She's there in the bower. I wish you joy of her."

With an inward sigh, she watched as Lord Dunmore came around the corner.

"Your grace," Dunmore said, stopping before her. "I simply wished to assure myself that you were well."

Clenching her fist, Perdita realized that she still had Archer's handkerchief. Schooling her features into a smile, she greeted Dunmore and tried to put Archer from her mind.

MANDA COLLINS GREW up on a combination of Nancy Drew books and Jane Austen novels, and her own brand of Regency romantic suspense is the result. An academic librarian by day, she investigates the mysteries of undergraduate research at her alma mater, and holds advanced degrees in English Lit and Librarianship. Her debut novel, *How to Dance with a Duke* spent five weeks on the Nielsen Bookscan Romance Top 100 list, was nominated for an RT Reviewer's Choice Award for best debut historical romance, and finaled in the Gayle Wilson Award of Excellence contest. She is a 2013 Winner of the Gayle Wilson Award of Excellence for her novella *The Perks of Being a Beauty*. She lives on the Alabama Gulf Coast with three cats, a dog, and always lots of books.

BOOKS BY MANDA COLLINS

How to Dance with a Duke | ISBN 9780312549244
How to Romance a Rake | ISBN 9780312549251
How to Entice an Earl | ISBN 9780312549268
The Perks of Being a Beauty | ISBN 9781466834903
Why Dukes Say I Do | ISBN 9781250023834
Why Earls Fall in Love | ISBN 9781250023841
Why Lords Lose Their Hearts | ISBN 9781250023865
Once Upon a Christmas Kiss | Coming Fall 2014

LENA DIAZ

"RIVETING!"
WENDY CORSI STAUB

ASHES, ASHES, THEY ALL FALL DEAD

AVON
IMPULSE

A DEADLY GAMES
THRILLER

What she doesn't remember ...

One by one the letters arrive at the FBI office in Savannah, Georgia. Inside, each bears a name--a victim of a twisted crime--and the singsong phrase Ashes, ashes, they all fall dead. Special Agent Tessa James becomes obsessed with finding the killer whose victims are crying out to her for justice.

Will kill her ...

When sexy, brilliant consultant Matt Buchanan is paired with Tessa to discover who's sending the "Ashes" letters, he discovers a serial arsonist who is leaving nothing but murder in his wake. Inexplicably, the clues point to Tessa herself, forcing her to realize that if she can't remember the forgotten years of her past, the name on the next letter will be hers.

ASHES, ASHES, THEY ALL FALL DEAD
BY LENA DIAZ

PROLOGUE

HOT, GREEDY TONGUES of flame licked around the eaves, teasing, tasting, like a new lover hungry for a first caress, ravenous to join with the tantalizing flesh of the woman lying inside the house.

The beckoning inferno drew him across the dew-laden grass until the heat was so intense he was forced to step back. He lifted his face to the sky as the first ashes fluttered down, brushing softly across his skin like a warm breath, a gentle kiss.

He captured the sooty flakes in his hands, the familiar, acrid scent making his nostrils flare. The comforting crackle of the fire subtly changed and he cocked his head to listen. No, the *fire* hadn't changed. Those were sirens, the high-pitched whine mingling with the dull roar of the flames.

He crushed the pieces of ash in his palms, picked up the gas can, and loped across the lawn to his truck. Too late. They were too late. They were *always* too late. And soon, he would have his revenge.

Ashes, Ashes, They All Fall Dead.

Chapter One

The stacks of letters cluttered the top of the conference room table, each one a bleak epitaph to a life stolen, a life lost, a life destroyed. FBI Special Agent Tessa James slid one of the pages toward her, gingerly running her latex-gloved finger across the words. A name—Sharon Johnson. So simple. So short. So inadequate. Beneath it, a killer's irreverent gloat, "Ashes, Ashes, They All Fall Dead," followed by an odd little curlicue, like someone would make when doodling, except that it was on every letter. It seemed obscene that his words, and his mark, sat on the same pages as his victims' names.

Even in death he wouldn't let them go.

The door opened, letting in a rush of air-conditioning that fluttered the pages across the brown laminate surface, like leaves scattering across a grave. Tessa slapped her hands down so the papers wouldn't fall off the table, and looked up to see her boss, Supervisory Special Agent Casey Matthews.

Wonderful.

At one time he'd been her biggest supporter and friend.

Not anymore.

He flicked a steely-gray glance at the tabletop. His mouth flattened and he shut the door behind him with an ominous click.

"Any new leads?" he asked.

The matter-of-fact tone of his voice didn't fool her. His ramrod-straight back and the tightness of his jaw were warning signs of an impending blowup. She mentally picked her way through a minefield of possible responses to his question. A cleverly constructed lie might save her. But she respected him too much to give him anything less than the truth.

"No new leads. I still haven't linked the names to any reported cases, besides the two we already knew about that weren't connected."

This time it was his turn to watch her, to weigh her words, to carefully select *his* response.

She met his gaze, unflinching. Defying him outright had never been her plan. Which was why she'd intended to have the forbidden letters back into evidence before he returned from his meeting across town. Either the meeting had ended early, or he'd been more suspicious than she'd realized and had come back specifically to see whether she was obeying his orders.

Unfortunately, she wasn't.

She wished it were as simple as just deciding to blindly follow his lead. But nothing about this situation was simple. There were real people behind each of the names on the letters, victims who deserved justice. Her colleagues had given up on the case long ago, but she couldn't. If life was even halfway fair, she wouldn't have to sneak around to fight for people she'd never even met. But life *wasn't* fair, and the FBI wasn't forgiving of agents who broke the rules.

"This has to be a hoax," he finally said. "It's been going on for, what, three years now? If someone had actually killed all these people and sent these letters to the FBI to taunt us about his crimes, we'd be able to match at least one of those names to an unsolved murder."

It always came down to the same argument. He thought it was a hoax. She was just as convinced it wasn't. She desperately wanted him to be right, because that would mean all those lives had *not* been lost. But, somehow, she *knew* this wasn't a joke. She knew it just as certainly as she knew she had to exert five-point-five pounds of pressure on her Glock 17's trigger to fire a shot. There was no doubt in her mind that whoever had sent the letters was deadly serious, a dangerous killer who had to be stopped.

"Tessa?"

She tore her gaze away from the forlorn collection of names. Agreeing with him would be the smarter path, the easier path.

But not the *right* path.

Regardless of what happened in the next few minutes, she wasn't going to cower and beg for forgiveness. *She* wasn't the one choosing budgets and resources over saving lives.

"It's not a hoax," she insisted. "It's been going on too long for that. We haven't alerted the media about the letters, so whoever sent them isn't getting any attention, or even the satisfaction of knowing he's made the FBI spend any time playing his game. There's no payoff."

Casey rested a hip against the table, half sitting. The rigidness of his posture eased, and he seemed to be truly considering her argument. "If the person sending these letters was typical, I'd agree with you. But it's just as likely he, or she, is mentally ill and gains enjoyment just by mailing them. Regardless, you have to look at the other side. Do the math. There have been twenty-three letters, which implies twenty-three victims, in less than thirty-six months—which is basically a fresh kill every six or seven weeks. His signature, his mode of killing, would have had to pop up on someone's radar by now. It's just not plausible that no one would have made the connection between at least some of his kills."

His logic was sound. If he was arguing about any other case, she'd agree with him. But this case, for some reason she couldn't fathom, struck her as different. She *had* to convince him she was right or more people would die.

She grabbed the first letter the killer had sent and held it up like an exhibit in court. "Anna Davidson. She's someone's daughter, maybe someone's mother or wife. Don't you want to know what happened to her? What about her family? Do they even know she's dead? Can you imagine the agonizing limbo they must be in, living each day wondering what happened and whether they'll ever see their loved one again?"

"You're assuming Anna Davidson is real. There's no proof that she is."

She let out a deep sigh of frustration and carefully matched the letter back to its envelope and replaced them on the stack.

"Can I prove she's real, that she was murdered? No. Not *yet*. But all I need is one clue to tie one victim to one of these names. A single thread I can pull and unravel this monster's game."

Casey crossed to the window. He pushed aside the blinds, but

Tessa knew he wasn't admiring the view. There *wasn't* one—unless he considered a narrow side street and concrete building interesting. The FBI field office was tucked a block back from Reynolds Square, as if to keep the modern building from blighting Savannah's historic district and ruining the tourists' pictures. No, he was thinking, trying to decide what to do about a defiant agent who'd disobeyed his direct orders one too many times.

He turned around and leaned back against the windowsill. "We have other cases."

Here it comes.

"We also have a cold-case unit," he continued, "which gave up on this months ago. When you asked for permission to work this case, my answer was clear. *No.* I need you on other assignments. And yet you continue to sneak around, working on what you want to work on instead of what you're supposed to work on."

She stiffened. "None of my other assignments have suffered in any way. The time I've spent on this has been on my own time, either during lunch or after hours."

He quite deliberately glanced at his watch, then looked at the clock on the far wall, which clearly showed it was mid-morning, not lunchtime.

Her face heated. "Okay, I admit that today—*for the first time*—I'm using regular work hours to examine the letters. But the only reason I decided to pull them out this morning is because I just wrapped up my last assignment and didn't have a new one to work on yet."

He rolled his eyes. "Right. Like you don't know what other pending cases we have and couldn't have started looking at one. We both know better. That's not the reason you took those letters out of evidence today and brought them in here."

Her frustration at his refusal to see reason warred with the need to try to placate him. She swallowed hard and carefully modulated her tone to sound respectful, even if her words were anything but. "I admit my decision was partially based on the fact that you were supposed to be in a meeting across town."

He let out a short bark of laughter. "You're not going to stop, are you? No matter how many times I order you to drop this, you're going to keep pressing, keep sneaking around." He held up a hand to halt her reply. "Don't answer that. It'll just piss me off."

His long strides quickly carried him across the small room, but instead of sitting, he paced back and forth. When he stopped directly in front of her, he flattened his palms on the top of the table and leaned down.

"What I want, what I need, is an explanation. Why is this case so important that you're risking an eight-year career? You and I both know you've worked twice as hard as most of the men in this office to prove yourself, to succeed in this old boys' network. You've built a reputation as one of the best agents on my team, and yet you're willing to throw all that away. Why? Why are you so . . . obsessed . . . with this case?"

The edge of steel flashing in his eyes, the harsh words about her throwing away her career, had her stomach sinking like a corpse weighted down with chains in the Savannah River. Had she pushed him too far? Was this the end of her career?

She tried to imagine a future as *Miss* Tessa James instead of *Special Agent* James. From the first time she'd seen an FBI agent on a TV show, chasing a bad guy, putting him away so he could never hurt anyone else again, she knew she'd grow up to do the same thing. She'd never have to rely on anyone else to protect her. *She* would be the one saving others. When she tried to imagine a future in which she wasn't an FBI agent, all she saw was a miserable, dark void.

"Well?" he pressed. "What is it about this case that has you willing to risk everything?"

She clutched her hands together beneath the table. Why was he dragging this out? Why not just fire her now and get it over with? If he were anyone else, she'd end this humiliation right now and walk out. But this was Casey. They'd been in the trenches together too many times. He'd earned the right to know why she'd done what she'd done. And this was the first time he'd ever specifically asked why this case was so important to her. Maybe he really cared, really wanted to know.

But how could she explain something she didn't understand herself?

Her shoulders slumped as the fight drained out of her. "I don't know, Casey. I wish I did. Maybe it's . . . maybe it's something about the names of the victims. Or maybe it's the 'Ashes, Ashes' thing he writes on the letters. There's something about that phrase that seems so . . . familiar."

He yanked the chair out across from her and straddled it. "Of course the Ashes, Ashes phrase sounds familiar. It's a nursery rhyme, or a bastardization of one. It's familiar to all of us."

They both sat silently, her dying inside, knowing she'd just destroyed her future. Him, looking more confused than angry as he drummed his fingers on the laminate tabletop.

His fingers stilled, and the sudden look of determination in his eyes immediately set her on edge. He'd just come to some kind of decision, and she knew before he spoke that she wasn't going to like it.

"I want the old Tessa James back," he said. "The one I could rely on to follow orders and work *with* me, instead of against me. The agent with promise and a brilliant career ahead of her. So, I'm not going to fire you. I'm not even going to reprimand you, even though you deserve it. But only if you'll give me something in return. You have to agree to a deal."

The hope that had begun to flare inside her when he started his little speech died a quick death. Casey wasn't the kind of man to make deals, so she couldn't imagine one where she'd come out the winner.

She eyed him warily. "What kind of deal?"

He waved his hand toward the pile of letters. "I'll give you one week, seven days, to prove this isn't a hoax and develop at least one solid lead—and I do mean solid, like granite. If at the end of that week you can't convince me this isn't a hoax, then you agree to drop this and never bring the letters up again."

She stared at him, stunned that he was giving her another chance, and even more stunned that he was going to let her do exactly what she'd wanted to do all along.

"You're going to *let* me work the case?"

He nodded. "For seven days. The clock starts tomorrow, day one. On day seven, game over. And you have to agree to my terms in writing."

The "in writing" part stung, but she'd broken his trust over the letters. It would take a long time to win it back.

"I'll take the deal, and I'll put it in writing." Blessed relief bubbled up inside her. She didn't know why he was being so accommodating, but she wasn't going to do anything that might make him rethink his decision. "You won't regret this, Casey. Without any other distractions, I'm sure I'll be able to—"

He held up his hand. "I'm not finished."

Her stomach sank again.

"There's one more requirement. I want you to have the resources you need so you can't complain later that I didn't give you the best possible chance to solve this thing. To that end, when

I go back to my office, I'm going to arrange for someone to help you."

Help her? *Wonderful.* Another partner. Her last one had been Pierce Buchanan. It had been a great partnership until they decided to date. Then his old flame, Madison, had come onto the scene and Tessa had foolishly thought she could get Pierce to choose her instead. She'd basically thrown herself at him, had kissed him, in fact, with his future wife watching through a window.

Not one of her prouder moments.

That had ended the partnership, and it had taken a while for her to feel comfortable working in the same office with him again without feeling like a fool. Taking on another partner, forcing someone to work on a cold case he had no interest in, wasn't exactly a great way to start a new partnership.

"I appreciate the offer." She struggled to keep the irritation from showing in her voice. "But I've already brainstormed with everyone in our office. I've followed up on every suggestion, but none of it amounted to even one new lead. There's no point in forcing me to work with another agent. It won't make a difference."

The tightening around his eyes told her she'd said too much. She belatedly realized she'd just thrown her fellow agents under the proverbial armored car by admitting they knew she'd been working on the letters case—and hadn't told him.

He crossed his arms over the back of his chair. "Wasting other agents' time on this isn't what I had in mind. I'm going to call a consultant, a local private investigator who specializes in working with law enforcement to solve cold cases. Then I want you to meet with him and explain the details of the case. Get him to agree to work on it with you. His name is Matt Buchanan."

She blinked and tried to form words several times before they finally came out. "Pierce's baby brother? You have to be kidding. He's, what, sixteen, seventeen?"

Her boss's knuckles whitened from clutching the back of the chair so hard.

Tessa immediately regretted her outburst, but her shock had driven all caution from her brain.

"I think he's twenty-four, not that it matters," Casey finally responded. "He's a brilliant investigator who's worked with several other agents in this office quite successfully. He holds master's degrees in both criminology and advanced mathematics with a minor in computer science. More importantly, in only three years he's helped close over *thirty* cold cases for seven different law-enforcement agencies, including ours. His solve ratio is eighty-five percent. What's the solve ratio for our cold-case unit?"

"More like twenty percent," she grudgingly admitted.

"Exactly."

He waited, as if he expected her to thank him and tell him how excited she was to work with a *child*. She'd had to put up with Matt's arrogant interference when he was still a college student, while Tessa was investigating Madison McKinley's abduction three years ago—the same Madison who eventually married Pierce. Tolerating Matt because he was Pierce's brother was one thing. But if Tessa was forced to actively work with him on an investigation, every day, for a solid week, she might as well go to jail right now.

Because she'd probably kill him.

Casey rapped one of his fists on the table. "Look, I know you have a problem with Matt, so I won't force you to work with him."

She cleared her throat, uncomfortable that her dislike of the man was so obvious. But she wasn't going to deny it either.

"It's your decision," Casey said. "But Buchanan is part of the deal. Work with him to develop that lead by day seven. If you're successful, this becomes an active investigation with my full support. No lead, the case is dead, and if I catch you even *thinking* about those letters again, your career is over."

ORIGINALLY FROM KENTUCKY, romantic suspense author Lena Diaz also lived in California and Louisiana before settling in northeast Florida with her husband, two children, and a Shetland Sheepdog named Sparky. A former Romance Writers of America Golden Heart® finalist, she won the prestigious Daphne du Maurier award for excellence in mystery and suspense and has been a finalist in the National Excellence in Romance Fiction Awards and the Bookseller's Best Awards. She loves to watch action movies, garden, and hike in the beautiful Tennessee Smoky Mountains. You can contact Lena through her website, www.LenaDiaz.com.

BOOKS BY LENA DIAZ

The Deadly Games Series
(HarperCollins/Avon Impulse)

He Kills Me, He Kills Me Not | ISBN 9780062114556
Simon Says Die | ISBN 9780062136329
Ashes, Ashes, They All Fall Dead | ISBN 9780062280886
Take the Key and Lock Her Up | ISBN 9780062280916

Harlequin Intrigue Books

The Marshal's Witness | ISBN 9781460304020
Explosive Attraction | ISBN 9781460312605
Undercover Twin | ISBN 9781460323144
Tennessee Takedown | ISBN 9781460325926
The Bodyguard | ISBN 9781460331880

RACHEL GRANT

WITHHOLDING EVIDENCE

Some secrets are worth dying for...

Military historian Trina Sorensen has a nearly impossible task before her: get recalcitrant but tempting former Navy SEAL Keith Hatcher to reveal what happened during a top secret Somalia op five years ago. Recent history isn't usually her forte, but the navy wants an historian's perspective and has given her the high security clearance to get the job done.

Keith isn't just refusing to tell Trina about the op, he's protecting a national secret that could destroy the lives of those he cares about the most. But not wanting to talk about a covert mission doesn't mean he isn't interested in spending time with the sexy historian, and the first time they kiss it's explosive.

When the past comes pounding on Keith's door, he'll do anything to keep Trina safe... Anything, that is, except tell her the secret that could get them both killed.

WITHHOLDING EVIDENCE
BY RACHEL GRANT

CHAPTER ONE

Falls Church, Virginia
August

TRINA SORENSEN STIFFENED her spine and rang the town house doorbell. She couldn't hear a chime, so after a moment of hesitation, she followed up with a knock. Seconds ticked by without any sound of movement on the other side. She rang the bell again, and then repeated the knock for good measure. The front door was on the ground floor, next to the garage. Glancing upward, she checked out the windows of the two upper floors. No lights on, but at nine in the morning on a hot August day in Falls Church, that didn't tell her anything. If the man she hoped to meet was home, he'd have to descend at least one flight of stairs, possibly two.

Patience.

She was about to ring the bell again when the door whipped open, startling her. She stepped back, then remembered she needed to project poise and straightened to meet her target's gaze.

Keith Hatcher was even more handsome in person than in his official navy photo, but she couldn't let that fluster her. It just meant he'd been blessed with good genes, a rather superficial measure of a person, really.

She took a deep breath and held out her hand. "Mr. Hatcher, Trina Sorensen, historian with Naval History and Heritage Command. I'd like to ask you a few questions about Somalia." She cringed as she said the last part. Too perky. Too eager. That was *not* how to approach a former navy SEAL when asking about a mission.

Sporting tousled dark hair that suggested he may have just

gotten out of bed, and wearing low-rise jeans and nothing else, the man leaned an impressive bare bicep against the doorframe and raised a quizzical thick eyebrow. "Trina? Cute name." He smiled. "It fits." He reached out and touched the top of her head. "But I think you should go back to the day care center you escaped from and leave me alone." He stepped back, and the door slammed shut.

She jolted back a step. He did *not* just pat her on the head and slam the door in her face.

Except that was exactly what Senior Chief Petty Officer Keith Hatcher had done.

She was aware she looked young, but dammit, she was thirty-one freaking years old—the same age as Hatcher. In fact, she was a few weeks *older* than him. She squared her shoulders and rang the bell again.

Seconds ticked by. Then minutes. She pounded with the side of her fist.

Finally the door opened. "Yes?" He leaned against the doorjamb again, this time stretching out an arm to touch the hinged side of the opening. His body language conveyed amusement mixed with annoyance.

"Senior Chief, I'm *Dr.* Trina Sorensen"—she never referred to herself with the pretentious title of doctor, but figured his crack about day care warranted it—"and I'm researching your SEAL team's work in Somalia five years ago for Naval History and Heritage Command and the Pentagon. You must answer my questions."

"Dollface, it's Sunday morning. The only thing I *must* do today is jack off."

She crossed her arms. "Fine. I can wait. It'll be what, one, maybe two minutes?"

The man tilted his head back and laughed. She saw her opportunity and ducked under his arm, entering, as she'd suspected, an enclosed staircase. The door to the left could only go to the garage. She went straight for the stairs, heading up to his home. Her heart beat rapidly at her own audacity, but she was never going to get the information she needed to do her job from the SEAL without taking risks.

"What the hell?" he sputtered, then added, "Who do you think you are, barging into my home?"

"I told you. I'm Dr. Trina Sorensen from NHHC," she

answered as she reached the landing that ended in the most spotless mudroom she'd ever seen. She crossed the room and stepped into his kitchen. Equally spotless. Either he had an amazing cleaning service, or he was a total neat freak. Given his disheveled appearance, she'd expected a disheveled home.

She leaned against a counter as he paused in his own kitchen doorway. His mouth twitched, but his jaw was firm, making her think he couldn't decide if he was annoyed or amused.

"I'll wait here while you masturbate. We can start the interview when you're done."

Amusement won, and a corner of his mouth kicked up. He took a step toward her. "It'll go faster if you help me."

Her heart thumped in a slow, heavy beat. Barging into his home might've been a mistake. She frowned. *Of course it was a mistake.* "I'm good to go. Already took care of business this morning in the shower. You go ahead without me."

He barked a sharp laugh, then shook his head. "What do you want, Dr. Sorensen?"

"As I said already, I'm here to ask you questions about Somalia." She pulled her digital recorder from her satchel. "Do you mind if I record our conversation?"

His brown eyes narrowed. "Hell, yes, I mind. More importantly, we aren't having a conversation. You are leaving. Now. Before I call the police."

"Please don't be difficult. I'm just doing my job."

"SEAL ops are classified." All hint of amusement left his voice, leaving only hard edges.

She sighed in frustration. Hadn't he bothered to read any of her e-mails? "I sent you what you need to verify my security clearance in my e-mail. And my orders came directly from the Pentagon."

"I don't give a crap if the pope sent you on orders from the president. I'm not telling you shit about a place I've never been."

He expected her to accept that and walk away? She'd never have gotten anywhere as a military historian if she allowed the men in her field to brush her off. "Oh, you've been to Somalia all right. You were there on a reconnaissance mission, gathering data about a rising al Qaeda leader who was taking advantage of a power vacuum created by ongoing interclan violence."

He crossed his arms and spoke softly. "I have no clue what you're talking about."

The man had a solid poker face; no hint that she'd surprised him with the paltry facts she knew. So he was handsome and big and had the most gorgeous sculpted pecs and abs she'd ever seen, and he was sharp to boot. "I'm researching various SEAL actions in Somalia over the last two decades, starting with Operation Gothic Serpent and ending with yours."

He cocked his head. "Who is your boss?"

"Mara Garrett, interim director of the history department at Naval History and Heritage Command."

His eyes widened when she said her boss's name. At last, a break in the poker face. Did he recognize Mara's name from her trouble in North Korea, her notorious run-in with Raptor, or because he knew Mara was married to the US Attorney General? Regardless, the name Mara Garrett opened doors, and Trina had one more threshold she wanted to traverse—from the kitchen to the living room, where she could conduct a proper interview.

"The work I did when I was in the navy is classified. Not only do I not have to tell you about an op I was never on in a country I've never visited, but I could also get in serious trouble if I *did* tell you a damn thing about the places I *have* been."

She handed him her card. "But you do have to answer me. The Pentagon wants this report. Your input is necessary." This project was her big break. Future naval operations could depend on her findings, and the biggest of the brass were eager for this account. She was already having visions of moving out of the cubicle next to cantankerous Walt. She could have walls. And a door.

"But, you see there, dollface, that's the problem. I'm not in the navy anymore. I don't take orders from the Pentagon. I don't have to follow commands from anyone, least of all a five-foot-nothing librarian who invaded my kitchen without my permission."

She straightened her spine and threw back her shoulders, determined to reach her full height. "I'm five foot three. And I'm an historian." Her glasses slipped, and she nudged them back to the bridge of her nose.

He chuckled, and she flushed. She'd have been better off if she hadn't corrected him on the librarian label as she adjusted her glasses.

"Whatever, doll. Listen, you have one minute to get out of my house, or I'm going to assume you've decided to watch me jerk off after all."

She couldn't look away from the brown eyes that held hers in a tense gaze. Just her luck that he was so frigging gorgeous. Attractive men made her self-conscious. Especially ripped, half-naked ones. "I'm not playing games, Senior Chief. I'm just here to do my job."

He smiled slowly and reached for his fly.

♆

KEITH LAUGHED AS the woman bolted down the stairs and out of his town house. He was sort of sorry to see her go, because that exchange had been fun—certainly worth getting out of bed for.

He waited until he heard the front door slam, then followed and locked the door. What kind of fool showed up at a guy's house at nine on a Sunday morning and expected him to be forthcoming about an op that was not only top secret but was also the single greatest and worst moment of his military career? As if he'd tell her—or anyone—about Somalia.

He'd been debriefed after the op. The people who needed to know what happened knew everything. It was enough for the powers that be, and it was enough for him.

He climbed the stairs and returned to his kitchen, where he made a pot of coffee. The woman—Trina—had been hot in a sexy, nerdy-librarian sort of way. There was probably a fancy name for the way she wore her hair in that twist at her nape, but to him it was a bun. And the little glasses with the red rims? Sexy as hell the way they slanted over her hazel eyes.

Did she dress the part of librarian on purpose, or was it some sort of weird requirement of her profession? It was too bad she hadn't decided to stay, because he had a hard-on after watching her march up his stairs in that straight skirt that cradled her ass.

He'd always had a thing for librarians—or historians—whatever.

If she had a PhD, she was probably a lot older than she looked. *Thank goodness.* Of course, she could be some sort of Doogie Howser genius.

Mug of coffee in hand, he headed into his office, woke his computer, and clicked on the mail icon. Had she really e-mailed him? It seemed like he'd have noticed.

New e-mail notifications came pouring in. Shit. How long had it been since he loaded e-mail? He checked the date of the first ones—from his dad, of course. These were nearly two weeks old. Oh yeah, he'd been so upset after the last round of antigovernment, antimilitary e-mails from his dear old dad, he'd turned off the mail program and took it out of start-up so it wouldn't run unless he initiated it. For some reason that had felt easier, less final, than blocking his father's e-mail address.

Thanks to the constant barrage of ranting messages, three months ago Keith had set his phone to only load e-mails from a select number of approved addresses. In the last two weeks, since he shut off mail on the computer, he'd received e-mails from the people who mattered to him on his phone, allowing him to forget he wasn't receiving everything on the computer.

He scanned the list, deleting the ones from his dad without opening any. Each time he tapped the button, he felt a twinge of guilt. It was time to block Dad once and for all. Yet he still refused to take that final step and wasn't quite sure why.

Misguided hope the man would change, he supposed.

After he'd deleted several e-mails, the name Trina Sorensen popped to the top of the list—the time stamp was last night. He scrolled down further and found four e-mails from her in the last week.

He opened her most recent message, noting the return address was indeed official navy. He scanned the contents. Huh. She'd told him that since he hadn't responded to her previous inquiries, she would be stopping by his house this morning, and if he didn't want her to show up, he should reply.

He lifted a finger to hit the Delete button and paused. Dammit. He owed her an apology.

Then he smiled, remembering that tight ass and those sexy calves. He'd liked the way she was quick with a comeback and didn't back down easily.

He wouldn't apologize via e-mail. He wanted talk to her in person so he could see her again. No way was he going to tell her about Somalia, but he could explain that in person too. Sort of.

Maybe his interest in the historian was only because he was bored. But at least she'd given him a reason to get out of bed this morning. Unemployment was for shit. He needed to *do* something.

An e-mail from his buddy Alec Ravissant reminded him of the garden party this afternoon at the home of Dr. Patrick Hill, the head of The MacLeod-Hill Exploration Institute in Annapolis, Maryland. Rav was running for the open Senate seat in Maryland, and the party was intended to introduce Rav to Hill's extensive connections in local politics and the military.

Hill's guests would be power-hungry high-society and military personnel. People who wanted to ingratiate themselves with military leaders, like the socialite made infamous in the Petraeus scandal a while back.

Sorry, Rav. No way in hell. Keith might be bored in his very early retirement, but he wasn't bored enough to attend a party that would require fending off the advances of married women while their husbands stood idly by, either oblivious, uncaring, or hoping their wives' infidelity would gain them admission into the centers of power.

Christ. He was starting to sound like his dad.

Just before he hit the Delete button, his eye caught the note at the bottom. Curt Dominick would be there, and Rav wanted to introduce them. Keith knew the US Attorney General had been the one to finally convince Rav to run for the Senate, so it was no surprise that Dominick would attend. He was both a power player and a good friend of Rav's. What gave Keith pause was realizing the man's wife, Mara Garrett—who happened to be sexy Trina the historian's boss—would probably attend as well.

Something Rav had said rang a bell—didn't the MacLeod-Hill Institute have some sort of oceanic-mapping joint venture with the navy? Specifically with the navy's underwater archaeology branch?

A quick Google search answered that question—yes—and revealed that the navy's underwater archaeology department was part of Naval History and Heritage Command.

Well, that changed everything. He'd lay odds everyone at NHHC with a connection to the MacLeod-Hill project had been invited to the party. This could be the perfect opportunity for Keith to apologize to the historian.

♆

FOUR-TIME GOLDEN Heart® finalist Rachel Grant worked for over a decade as a professional archaeologist and mines her experiences for storylines and settings, which are as diverse as excavating a cemetery underneath an historic art museum in San Francisco, survey and excavation of many prehistoric Native American sites in the Pacific Northwest, researching an historic concrete house in Virginia, and mapping a seventeenth century Spanish and Dutch fort on the island of Sint Maarten in the

Netherlands Antilles.

She lives in the Pacific Northwest with her husband and children and can be found on the web at www.Rachel-Grant.net.

Books by Rachel Grant

 Concrete Evidence
(Evidence Series #1)

 Body of Evidence
(Evidence Series #2)

 Withholding Evidence
(Evidence Series #3)

 Grave Danger

Midnight Sun (Novella in Twelve Shades of Midnight anthology – coming October 2014)

KRISTA HALL

BROKEN PLACES

GOLDEN HEART® WINNER

She's on a mission to change lives

When one of her students becomes the latest victim of a D.C. gang-slaying, sociology professor Trevy Barlow is determined to protect the other girls in her literacy class for at-risk teens—even if it means compromising her own safety.

He's on a short clock to find a killer

FBI gang task force agent Cruz Larsen isn't about to let Trevy endanger herself or sidetrack his investigation with her do-gooder meddling. But when a key witness refuses to talk to anyone except her, Cruz has to find a way to earn her trust so that she'll play by his rules.

Now a sadistic predator is after them

For Cruz, keeping Trevy safe has become more than a duty—his heart is involved too. But all of his leads have flatlined. And he's beginning to suspect that a hidden third party has rekindled the gang rivalry for reasons far beyond a D.C. turf war. Caught in the crossfire, Trevy will have to risk it all to give them a fighting chance to survive.

Broken Places
by Krista Hall

Prologue

Sunday, February 16

LOLA SANCHEZ LEANED over the open trunk as she pulled the last hundred-dollar bill from her waistband and crammed it into a slit along the rim of the spare tire. Then she tugged her shirt—really more of a stretchy floral tent—over the bulk of her belly and tried to close her jacket against the frigid air of the dimly lit parking garage.

It was hardly worth the effort. At eight months pregnant, there was little difference in her girth now than when the money had been stuffed down the front of her maternity pants, and the edges of her jacket still wouldn't meet. Spring was only a few weeks away, though, so soon it wouldn't matter. With a sigh of impatience, she flipped the tire to hide the slit.

The spare was heavier, but not noticeably so. Ten thousand dollars—one hundred worn, green bills—didn't weigh much. Lola secured the tire in the wheel well and shut the trunk of the dull orange BMW. The sound echoed in the deserted parking garage beneath the New Hope Community Center on the eastern edge of the District of Columbia. At ten minutes past eight, she was alone. Her money was safe.

Eager to be on her way before the security guard's routine after-hours sweep of the parking garage, Lola fingered the key on the long pink velvet ribbon she wore around her neck. She slipped the makeshift necklace over her head and unlocked the driver side door of the old coupe. Her back ached. Her toes were little blocks of ice in her fake leather shoes. She longed to be in her room, snuggled under the covers of the bed she shared with her sister. Warm and safe.

But not yet. Bandit would be waiting at the side door of the community center. She was already late, and if she didn't show up soon, he might come looking for her. That would be almost as bad as getting caught by the center's rent-a-cops. She had to hurry.

She ducked her head through the loop of velvet and settled the cold key between her heavy breasts. Lola tugged the driver's seat forward so she could lean into the back and reach underneath it with the flat of her hand. Her fingers closed on the cold s-shaped curves of exposed springs, but that was all she felt.

Where is it? An icy trickle of unease slithered down her spine. She couldn't let Bandit go to Razor empty-handed.

The harsh squeak of brakes, echoing in the dead air of the parking garage, startled her. She pushed the seat back into place as quickly as she could, but was still wedged in the open doorway when a black sedan glided to a stop behind the BMW, blocking her in.

The passenger side window lowered with a hushed hum of sound. "Looking for something?" The rough voice brushed over Lola, raising tiny goose bumps on her arms.

The ominous click of the car door opening sent Lola scrambling out of the old clunker as fast as her bulk would allow. *Don't panic*, she told herself, straightening to her not very impressive height of five feet. A stranger wouldn't know that this wasn't her car. A stranger wouldn't know she was a thief and a liar.

Lola pasted a smile on her face. Everyone wanted to help a pregnant woman, especially one who was barely seventeen. She pushed her dark hair out of her eyes.

"Everything's fine," she said, willing the stranger to stay in his car and drive away. Pronto. There was still that rent-a-cop to worry about. And Bandit. *Go away, go away*, she silently chanted as if repeating the words over and over might give them power.

She heard the soft scrape of shoes against the concrete floor.

"Everything is not fine," the stranger said as he circled the front of his car and walked toward her, slow but steady. The hood of his gray parka was pulled low over his face, and his hands were gloved. Everything about him spoke of menace. "Did you think I wouldn't notice?"

She took one step back and then another.

"Do I know you?" She tried to make out his features, but they were hidden in shadow. *Run.* The thought came from somewhere deep inside her. It was the same instinct that had cautioned her not to tell anyone, not even Bandit, about her secret stash. She swiveled her head, searching for an escape route.

The elevator and stairs were a hundred yards behind her. Clutching her swollen belly, she made a sudden lunge forward, knocking the stranger off balance with her shoulder. Then she pivoted on her heels, her long hair fanning out like a banner. She raced toward the stairs.

"*Mierda*," she heard him grunt as he came rushing after her.

Her fear gave her speed, but he was faster. The sound of his rapid footsteps pounding against the concrete floor was her only warning before he grabbed her by the hair, the sting of pain bringing tears to her eyes.

With a feral sound of desperation, she jerked her head forward, leaving a hank of long black hair hanging from his tightly fisted hand. Ignoring the tearing pain, she ran faster, straining against the solid weight of the baby that slowed her down.

A few more steps. The door to the stairs was almost within reach. *Keep going. Don't stop now.* If she could just get to the fire alarm on the other side of the door, she could set it off and then the security guard who patrolled the community center would head down to the garage to investigate. Breathing hard, she gripped the cold metal door handle with both hands and pulled with all her might.

It was locked.

She only had an instant to feel the sickening slide of fear, and then the stranger was on her, trapping her against the door, smashing the tight melon of her belly against the unyielding metal. She couldn't think, couldn't move, couldn't breathe.

His gloved fingers brushed against her throat as he grabbed the key on the pink ribbon she wore around her neck, and lightly scraped its serrated edge against the flesh of her cheek. A promise of pain.

"Where's the money?"

Shock held her silent.

"Tell me, *puta*." The quick tap of metal against her temple was the only warning before he slashed the sharp point of the key across her forehead, leaving jagged cuts.

She bit down on the cry that swelled in her throat along with the temptation to give him what he wanted. She couldn't let him take her baby's money. She had worked too hard for it, risked too much.

"Where?"

Warm trails of blood snaked down her face. The ribbon tightened, and black spots crowded the edge of her vision.

The low rumble of the elevator as it descended from the main floor of the New Hope Community Center saved her from answering. The security guard was on his way at last. Her attacker heard it too. The ribbon eased. Inhaling in harsh, heavy sobs, Lola sagged against the door. He would run now.

Heat poured off him, burning her back where he pressed against her. He leaned his head closer to hers, tightening the ribbon again, choking her. She tried to free her hands, but he was still holding her against the door.

"I'll get it back," he whispered in Lola's ear.

The elevator groaned to a halt. Soon the double doors would slide open. Why wasn't he letting her go? His warm breath brushed against her face. Did he want to get caught?

Fueled by desperation, she turned her head in an attempt to loosen his grip. Her lips slid along the hard edge of his jacket zipper and caught on a scratchy square of Velcro. If she could figure out who he was, maybe she'd know how to get him to leave her alone. She raised her eyes and met his gaze.

Then he jerked the ribbon tighter.

Chapter One

Sunday, February 16

"*¡CHINGAZOS LOCOS!*" THE muffled cry from the hallway filtered into the overheated classroom in the New Hope Community Center, drowning out the quiet squeak of marker against whiteboard. Trevy Barlow turned, marker in hand, as more sounds bombarded the room—running feet and the crackle of a police radio. Ten pairs of eyes darted to the window set in the closed door at the back of the room.

"Wait here," Trevy said, forcing herself to sound calmer than she was. "I'll find out what's going on."

On her way to the back of the room, Trevy smiled reassuringly at the teenage girls an instant before the door swung open and a dark-haired teenage boy careened into her. She fell back against an empty desk as a District of Columbia policeman barreled into the room after him, gun drawn.

"Hey! There's no need for that," Trevy protested, her heart firmly lodged in her throat. "This is a classroom."

"*¿Dónde está?*" the teen demanded, his dark eyes searching the faces of the girls, who had all risen from their chairs by now. Their alarmed chatter filled the room. Trevy realized that she recognized him. He was the boyfriend of one of her no-show students, Lola Sanchez.

"*¿Bandit, qué pasa?*" one of the girls called out to him.

He ignored her and fixed his gaze on Trevy. "*¿Dónde está Lola?*"

Trevy slowly backed away from the teenager, who looked wild-eyed with panic. One of the girls in the room said in rapid-fire Spanish, "Lola didn't come tonight. We thought she was with you."

"*Sí, sí,*" a chorus of agreement sounded behind Trevy.

"I was supposed to meet her before class, but I was late," Bandit answered in Spanish. He grabbed Trevy's arm. "*¿Dónde está?*" Where is she?

Before she could reply, the policeman yanked Bandit away. Trevy was relieved to see he had holstered his gun. Relieved, that is, until he pushed Bandit face first into the wall. Hard.

"Careful," Trevy said. "Don't hurt him."

"Hold still," the policeman grunted, ignoring her. He handcuffed Bandit's wrists with a plastic restraint. Then he keyed his radio. "Runner secured. He entered the building through a propped-open fire door on the east side. I'm on the main level. Third room on the left."

"Hey! ¡*Páralo!*" Stop it, the girls protested. They crowded in behind Trevy.

The policeman glanced over his shoulder at them, his face a hard, pale oval beneath his hat.

"Quiet," he snapped, his mouth set in a line. He shoved Bandit into a chair. "Sit." He keyed his radio again. "I got ten teenage girls here, and a woman—" he paused to assess Trevy "—late twenties, early thirties. They know the gangbanger."

"Take names and hold 'em till Larsen gets there," came the static-filled reply. "He'll want to talk to them."

"Ten-four." He cut his eyes to Trevy. "You in charge?" His hand rested on the holster of his gun, an unspoken threat.

"What has he done?" Trevy cast a worried glance at the teenager who sat slumped on a metal chair, his face turned away from her, all of the fight drained out of him. Her eyes caught on the tattoo of a clenched fist, dark against the smooth skin of his neck. The gang symbol of Chingazos Locos. The girls shifted restlessly behind her. She could feel their fear pulsing against her like a living thing.

"Just answer the question," the policeman said. "Are you in charge?"

"Yes. Trevania Barlow. I teach a literacy class for high school dropouts," she said, carefully neglecting to mention the girls' gang affiliation with Chingazos Locos. "The community center lets me use this classroom on Sunday evenings."

"I'll need to see some identification."

Dropping her gaze to the nameplate pinned on his dark blue jacket opposite the gold badge with the Metropolitan Police Department logo, she said, "My driver's license is in my bag, Officer Janklow." Then she pointed toward a large leather satchel in the corner near the whiteboard.

"Get it," he said, before shifting his glance to the nervous herd of teenagers standing behind her. "The rest of you, back to your desks."

The girls ignored him and followed Trevy to the front of the classroom.

"Wait here," she told them before returning to the policeman and handing him her license.

Officer Janklow jotted down her contact information in a small notebook he pulled from his jacket pocket. "How about him," he said, jerking his chin toward Bandit. "What's his name?"

"Bandit."

"His real name."

Trevy studied the officer for a moment, debating how forthcoming she should be. She shrugged. "Ask him."

Janklow's mouth tightened. "You don't know his real name?"

"There's no reason I would, Officer," she said, sidestepping the question. "He's just the boyfriend of one of my students."

The officer gave a small snort of disbelief and rubbed a hand across his forehead. "All right, Ms. Barlow. Let's move on to the girls. You must know their names."

The girls tittered nervously. She could sense one or two of them were ready to bolt from the room. They were afraid. In their world, the police were the enemy.

"Why do you need their names?"

"Let's start with her."

He pointed directly at Rosa. Of course he would choose one of the girls who was undocumented. And on the verge of panicking—Trevy could tell from the way she had sidled away from the others to better position herself for escape.

"I don't remember," Trevy said, lying without hesitation. She wasn't sure she trusted Officer Janklow not to detain Rosa, even though it was unlikely the teen was mixed up in the trouble Bandit had been running from.

"You don't remember!" Officer Janklow slammed a fist on the table. He stalked across the room. "What's your name?"

"*No hablo inglés*," Rosa said in a quavering voice.

"I don't believe this." He jammed a hand on his hip. "How about you?" He looked at Angel, who stood next to Rosa.

Angel shrugged and raised her eyebrows in a parody of confusion. "*¿Qué?*"

"I've had enough of this bull." Janklow unsnapped his holster and fingered the handle of his gun.

It was an empty threat, Trevy told herself. But her heart rate increased just the same, fear settling in her stomach like a lump of ice.

"Each and every one of you is going to tell me your name and address."

"Why do you need that information?" Trevy asked again. "We haven't done anything wrong."

"If you don't cooperate, then we'll have to go down to the police station to straighten this out."

As if it had been choreographed, the girls all raced for the door at the same time.

Officer Janklow swore under his breath and drew his gun. "Nobody move!"

"Put your gun away," Trevy shouted over the din. She positioned herself between the officer and the stampeding girls. "Can't you see you've frightened them?"

On the verge of losing control, he waved his gun at her midsection. "Get out of my way!"

"Put the gun away, and they won't try to run," Trevy said even though she knew the gun hadn't fazed them. His threat of a visit to the police station had done that. Still, they'd all be a lot safer once Officer Janklow holstered his weapon.

The girls already had the door open, Rosa in the lead, when they suddenly pulled back. Another frightened murmur rippled through the group. They huddled closer together, giving Trevy an unobstructed view of the doorway. And of the man who stood there, filling the space with his powerful presence.

One glance explained why her students had frozen in place. It wasn't just his height or the breadth of his shoulders that made him so intimidating, but the tightly leashed energy that seemed to hum just beneath the surface of his skin. His black hair was a touch too long and a couple of days of stubble shadowed his hard jaw. Even the herringbone sport coat he was wearing—a half-hearted stab at respectability?—did little to soften the effect of his black T-shirt, faded jeans, and take-no-prisoners stare.

"Going somewhere, ladies?" His voice was deceptively soft, but it had more power to sway than the other man's gun.

Only Officer Janklow seemed immune. "About time you got here, Larsen. Things are going to hell."

Larsen's sharp gaze took in the room, a quick survey that seemed to miss nothing. "Put the gun away," he said with a quiet menace that was impossible to ignore.

Janklow scowled, but did as he was told. "If you can believe it, nobody in this room appears to speak English. Except for Ms. Barlow." He stabbed a finger in her direction. "And so far, she doesn't seem to know anyone's name except for her own. Oh, and his."

"Really." Larsen raised a dark brow. "Well, that's something, isn't it?" he said. Trevy thought she could detect the trace of a West Texas drawl. "What's his name?"

"Bandit."

"Bandit?"

"That's *all* Ms. Barlow can recall." Janklow's voice was heavy with sarcasm.

Trevy ignored Officer Janklow and moved closer to this man called Larsen. He outranked the patrolman, that much was obvious. She didn't know whether that was good or bad. The new guy seemed like a hard-ass, but at least he wasn't waving a gun around like a lunatic. She and the girls had done nothing wrong, so they didn't deserve to be treated like criminals. Her glance cut from Bandit to the girls, who had regrouped by the whiteboard.

Larsen held his ground in the open doorway, effectively blocking the girls' escape route. His measuring gaze touched on Bandit before settling on Trevy. She opened her mouth to complain about Officer Janklow's outrageous behavior, but couldn't find the words. She was thrown off by his narrowed eyes. They were the color of pale green jade, cold and intense, all the more startling in contrast to the straight black brows that were arrowing downward in disapproval.

"Ms. Barlow?" he asked.

"Yes, Trevania Barlow. Who are you?"

His impenetrable façade slipped for an instant, his eyes showing a quick flash of surprise. And then, just as quickly, his shuttered expression was firmly back in place.

"Special Agent Larsen, ma'am." He pulled identification out of his jacket pocket and handed it to her.

"Diego Cruz Larsen," she read aloud for the benefit of the girls, who were watching her from the front of the room with a mixture of hope and fear in their eyes. They were counting on her to protect them. "FBI."

Interesting name, she couldn't help but think as she handed back his badge. Of course, the blending of cultures was as American as apple pie, baseball, and fireworks on the Fourth of July. She wondered what had brought an FBI agent to the community center on Sunday night. His unshaven face and casual attire spoke volumes. He hadn't planned on working this evening.

With a careless motion, doubtless one he'd made a thousand times before, he clipped his ID on the pocket of his jacket. "I'm with the Metro Area Gang Task Force," he said in a low voice, taking Trevy's arm and moving her out into the deserted hallway. "I'd appreciate your cooperation in this matter."

"Ms. Barlow doesn't know the meaning of the word cooperation," Janklow muttered under his breath as he took over Agent Larsen's position in the open doorway.

"I don't cooperate with gun-toting lunatics," Trevy retorted.

The tightening of his fingers on her arm was the only indication that Agent Larsen was annoyed by their sparring. His voice was deceptively calm when he said to Janklow, "It's Doctor Barlow."

"What?" Janklow replied, voicing the same one-word question that was bouncing around in Trevy's head.

"Dr. Trevania Barlow is a sociology professor at George Washington University. An expert on Latino gangs."

So, Agent Larsen was familiar with her work? He probably had no idea how much that meant to her. It was rare for her to get any acknowledgment outside of academic circles. Even rarer for someone in law enforcement to know her by reputation.

"You teach at GW?" Janklow asked her as if Agent Larsen might be trying to trick him.

"That's right."

"She also studies gangs in their natural habitats," Agent Larsen said, turning to Janklow, "and then writes books with weighty titles like *The Influence of Cultural Roots on Gang Formation*. The chapter on Latino gang symbols is a must-read." He glanced at her. "Are you here for more research, Dr. Barlow?"

"Research?" She tugged her arm free of his grasp, stung by the implication that she was using her students to further her academic career.

"This class is not about research," she said through clenched teeth. "These young women want to improve their reading skills and prepare for the GED. The school system has failed them. Miserably. I couldn't stand by without trying to do something about it."

"And then you'll write a book about it," he said, unconvinced. "A memoir if you're aiming for the bestseller lists."

"Pretty hard to pass the GED if you don't know English," Officer Janklow smirked.

"It's offered in Spanish," Trevy said, hands fisted on her hips. She turned her glare to Janklow. And then Larsen. "What's wrong with you? We haven't broken any laws. Why are you harassing us?"

The patrolman stared straight ahead, conveniently deaf and dumb.

"Coward," Trevy muttered under her breath.

"Shut the door, Janklow." Agent Larsen waited until the door clicked into place, then he turned to Trevy. "There's a dead girl in the parking garage."

KRISTA HALL WON the 2013 Golden Heart® Award for Broken Places. She lives in the mid-Atlantic with her husband and children and newest writing companion-a chocolate Lab puppy named Rosie. She can be found online at www.kristahall.com and on the group blog www.kissandthrill.com.

BOOKS BY KRISTA HALL

Broken Places | ISBN: 9780990360810

A
MEN OF
STEELE
NOVEL

GWEN
HERNANDEZ
AWARD-WINNING AUTHOR
BLIND FURY

SHE'S DESPERATE TO LEARN THE TRUTH

When always-play-it-safe Jenna Ryan starts questioning how her brother died in Afghanistan, someone decides she must be stopped. Permanently. Her brother's best friend—a sexy thrill-seeker she can't stop thinking about—won't reveal what he knows about the fatal shoot-out, putting Jenna at odds with the only man she trusts to keep her alive.

THE TRUTH IS THE ONE THING HE CAN'T GIVE HER

Former special forces operator Mick Fury would give his life to keep his best friend's irresistible sister safe. He took an oath to stay silent about their last mission, but Mick's will is tested by the white-hot attraction to Jenna he's tried to ignore for years. Now he must risk everything—even falling in love—to protect her from the truth that could destroy them both.

Blind Fury
by Gwen Hernandez

Chapter One

IN THE LAND of dust and sand, things got messy when it rained. Mick Fury's boots made sucking sounds in the mud left behind by a morning shower as he strode along the graffiti-covered blast wall that ran the perimeter of Kandahar Airfield.

He kept pace with Rob Ryan, ignoring the kerosene scent of jet fuel assaulting his nose as they headed to meet up with their Claymore Security teammates. They were scheduled to train local police recruits in tactical shooting techniques today. A worthy exercise if the trainees stayed alive long enough to use their new skills. Unfortunately, cops in Afghanistan were one of the Taliban's favorite targets.

Rob waggled a large rip-proof envelope addressed to his sister in Virginia. "Let me drop this in the mail on our way."

They detoured to the makeshift post office. "Did I forget Jenna's birthday or something?" Mick asked.

"Have you ever remembered it?" Rob ribbed him.

Actually, he had. Every year. November twenty-fifth.

"No," Rob said when he didn't answer. "It's just some notes and stuff that I don't have room for in my bag."

"So you're really not coming back?" A lead weight settled on Mick's chest. He and Rob had been best friends and teammates for twelve years. They'd had each other's backs through boot camp, pararescue training, and now at Claymore. If Rob left in two weeks like he planned, then Mick would be left here with only his friend Dan Molina and a bunch of assholes, the kind who thrived in an industry where the rules of civilization didn't apply.

The brotherhood he'd experienced in the Air Force—putting the members of the team above all else—had been hard to find in the world of private security contracting. Any one of them could walk away at any time, and some of the guys were outright criminals who'd never be allowed to carry a gun in the States.

"I'm really not coming back," Rob said, stuffing the envelope into a slot in the shipping containers that masqueraded as a post office. "And you shouldn't either."

It was an old argument. The constant stress, the poor management, and the barren surroundings chafed like a tight shoe. But there was no substitute for the adrenaline rush. There was something about cheating death that made him feel alive like nothing else could.

"What else can I do?" Mick asked. "Every time we go home, I'm happy for about two weeks. And then it all starts to seem so pointless, so boring." And quiet. There was nothing worse than being left alone with his thoughts. At least here in this hellhole he knew without a doubt that he was good for something.

Rob shoved his hands in his front pockets and rubbed a heel in the mud while they waited for the others to show up. "You think I don't feel the same way? But every time I leave, the look in Jenna's eyes nearly rips my heart out. I can't do that to her anymore."

Mick knew that look. Had memorized it long ago, along with everything else about the one woman who was off limits to him...and not just because Rob had threatened to permanently end his sex life if he tried anything.

He couldn't toy with the heart of a woman who'd suffered so much already. Jenna was the kind of girl you married and took home to Mom. Not Mick's usual type. She was smart and sweet, hardly a seductress. But somehow he couldn't get her pale, almost-gray eyes and schoolgirl freckles out of his head.

"What will you do?" he asked Rob, bringing himself back to the ugly reality of Afghanistan. "I can't see you settling down to a desk job and a white picket fence."

Rob laughed, but the humor didn't reach his eyes. "Screw that. I was talking to Dan, and he knows a guy who's a flight medic for one of those MedEvac helicopters. They also do search and rescue missions. I'll have to go to school first, but it'll be worth it. It will be like being in the PJs again, but without anyone shooting at you."

"Then where's the thrill?" Mick asked, not entirely joking. He plastered on his trademark carefree smile and tapped his rifle. He never should have left pararescue, but the money he'd been offered to join Claymore had been impossible to resist.

His friend shook his head. "Just think about it, okay?"

"Sure." He'd think about it. In fact, he already thought about it almost daily. Jesus, why couldn't he be normal? When he was here, he wanted to go home—drive his new Camaro, flirt with girls, party with his friends; and when he was back in Virginia he could hardly stand it. The tedium and pettiness of Stateside life was suffocating. At least things made sense here.

His job was to survive. Simple as that.

"Hey." Rob grabbed Mick's arm as a large armored vehicle rumbled past, leaving deep grooves in the mud. "Promise me one thing." He looked way too serious for Mick's taste. Even more serious than usual.

"What's that?"

"If something happens to me, you'll leave Claymore and take care of Jenna."

Oh, hell no. They were not going to have this conversation. Not right before going outside the wire. He bounced his eyebrows at Rob and forced a smile. "Take care of her, huh?"

"Yeah, and that includes protecting her from guys like you." Rob ran a hand through his close-cropped hair. "Come on, man. I mean it. I'll feel better knowing that she wouldn't be left alone."

"We've been here for two years. Why are you asking me this now?" Mick wrinkled his nose as the wind shifted, bringing with it the pungent odor of the sewage treatment plant—aka The Poo Pond. "Did something happen?"

Rob glanced around and shook his head with feigned indifference that didn't fool Mick for a second. "No, I'm just being, you know, superstitious now that I've given my notice. If I don't leave any loose ends, then nothing will happen."

He was full of crap, but Mick let it go. "Dude, you don't even have to ask. She's the closest thing I have to a sister of my own."

Except for the very un-brotherly thoughts he had about her. "But you're the one who's going to be there for her, so it doesn't matter. You're going to go home, find a job, get a dog, and meet a girl. In another year, I won't recognize you. You'll probably even own a minivan." Mick pulled a face, like he couldn't imagine a worse fate.

Rob's shoulders visibly relaxed and the line between his eyebrows softened. What the hell was going on with him? He'd never been this tightly wound before.

"Thanks. I owe you one."

Mick consulted his palm as if it were a notebook, and pretended to cross something out. "By my calculations, that makes us even." He grinned. "Hell, if I'd known you were this easy to get square with, I would have offered months ago."

Rob finally laughed, and the knot in Mick's chest loosened.

"Hey, ladies. You ready to run the gauntlet?" Three of their crew trudged toward them, nine millimeters in their thigh holsters and M4s strapped to their chest rigs, always at the ready. Dressed in khaki pants and polo shirts, they looked like an army of muscle-bound frat boys.

Mick and Rob fit right in.

"As long as you brought your diapers this time, Beavis," Mick called out, using the nickname the man had earned for his rat-like resemblance to the animated character. "I don't want shit to get all over the seats if we take fire."

Beavis flipped him off and they walked toward their armored vehicles to meet up with the rest of the group for the briefing.

Just another day in paradise.

AN HOUR LATER, Mick dropped to his knees in the mud next to Rob. "No, no, no!" He tore at his friend's mangled body armor and sticky, wet shirt and—oh God, *no*. He spread his hands over the ragged mess that used to be his friend's chest, as if he could hold him together by magic. His skills as a medic were of no use to him with an injury this bad... All he could do was try to stop the alarming flow of blood. "Damn it, Rob, hang on for me. You're going home, remember? Come on, *come on*."

Fucking Murphy and his law. Rob should have known better than to announce that he was going home right before they went outside the wire. Everyone knew a convoy was an easy target for roadside bombs and insurgent attacks.

Today, they'd managed to find both.

This can't be happening. Mick adjusted his position and pressed harder. Rob couldn't die; he was one of the good ones. Jenna needed her brother.

Mick needed him.

"Jenna," Rob whispered, clutching weakly at Mick's arm. His look said he knew he wouldn't make it.

Mick blinked against the burn of hot tears and nodded. "Don't worry. I'll watch out for her until you're on your feet again. Just stay with me." But the blood wouldn't fucking stop. It bubbled through his fingers, warm and sticky and relentless.

Rob closed his eyes and mumbled.

Mick leaned close to hear him over the noise of engines, men shouting, and the buzzing in his ears left by the ricochet of gunfire. "What's that?"

"Don't tell her."

Sharp smoke stung his nose as Mick surveyed the carnage surrounding them. The barren ground was covered with lifeless figures slicked with mud and blood. He closed his eyes briefly to block out the images, but like so many other horrors he'd witnessed, the scene would haunt him forever.

No way in hell would he ever want to talk about it. Keeping this horrific moment from Jenna was an easy promise to make. "Never."

JENNA RYAN COULDN'T remember the last time she'd been so full of hope. She used her running shirt to wipe the sweat from her face and filled a glass with cold water from the door of her refrigerator. According to the clock on the microwave, she didn't need to leave for two more hours. Even then she'd probably be early for her interview, but it was always better to play it safe with traffic in the D.C. area.

She perched on the arm of the sofa in her living room and drank the icy water, letting the scent of vanilla from her favorite plug-in air freshener calm her jumpy nerves as her body cooled. Her lips curved into a smile when she looked at one of the pictures on the fireplace mantle. Dressed in desert camouflage and holding large rifles in front of an armored truck, her brother Rob and his best friend Mick stared down at her.

Rob was going to be so happy for her if she got this new database analyst job. It wasn't the self-employment route he'd been pushing her to try, but Travers & West would be a huge improvement over her current employer. And interviewing for a new job was just about all the stress she could handle until he was home safe.

An hour later, showered and dressed, she reviewed her resumé one more time and practiced her answers to potential interview questions. After three years of putting up with the jerks at Quicksilver Defense Systems—QDS for short—she wanted to be as prepared as possible for the job that could be her ticket out.

Travers & West had a reputation for treating its employees well, offering flexible hours and performance-based bonuses. What a nice change that would be. And if she got the job, Rob could quit worrying about her and focus on himself.

And they both needed *that*.

Her cell phone rang as she was loading her breakfast dishes in the dishwasher.

"Are you ready?" Jenna's best friend, Tara Fujimoto, asked in her high-pitched voice.

"Yep. As long as I don't pass out from nerves. But I'm feeling better after Rob's call yesterday." He and Mick had called to wish her luck, knowing she would need encouragement.

"And did you talk to Mick too?"

"Yes." Jenna couldn't keep the exasperation out of her voice. As usual, he'd made a point of talking to her before Rob ended the call. Mick had told her once that he needed a little bit of normal every once in a while. He didn't have a sister to call, so he borrowed Jenna.

"I think he likes you," Tara said.

"As a surrogate sister, maybe." If she tried hard enough, she could convince herself that she saw him as a brother. The man hiding beneath the reckless playboy facade had always tempted her, but she couldn't risk her already fragile heart.

Tara snorted. "Hardly."

"How Mick Fury thinks of me is irrelevant. I'd never get involved with a guy who goes through women like I go through tissues."

"Don't you mean he *blows* through them?" Tara chuckled.

Jenna groaned. "Can we talk about something else? Like the fact that Rob is finally coming home?"

Tara went silent for a beat, no doubt trying to rein in a sarcastic comment. "For how long?"

"For good." The words danced on Jenna's tongue and she found herself bouncing on her toes like a little girl at Christmas waiting to open her gifts.

"That's great," Tara said evenly.

"I think he really means it this time." Jenna leaned against the cool countertop. Somehow she would find a way to make him happier, a way to convince him to stay. "He was talking about going back to school and adopting a rescue dog. It sounds like he's given it a lot of thought."

"Well, good. Maybe that will make up for having Carl on your case all the time."

Jenna covered her ears. "Ack, no. I don't want to talk about my boss right before my interview. Besides, if things go well, Carl will be history." Though if he found out she'd used a personal day to go on a job interview, she might be history at QDS whether the interview went well or not.

"You're right. You're going to be great today and we'll never have to talk about that jerk again." Tara giggled. "Let's talk about Mick instead."

"Tara!"

Her friend gave a dramatic sigh. "Fine. I'm glad you're looking for a new job, even though it'll be lonely here without you around. But are you sure you wouldn't be happier working for yourself? From what I hear, programmers are in high demand. Finding work should be a piece of cake."

A pipe dream. Wishful thinking. "You sound like Rob. He even offered to front me the money when he gets back." No matter how much the private security company he worked for paid him, she didn't want to take him up on the offer. She couldn't risk losing the money. Not when he'd literally dodged bullets to earn it.

"Do it," Tara said, her voice filling with excitement. "You're hard-working, conscientious, and super smart. You'll make a killing."

Jenna's chest squeezed. Easy for her friend to say. "I appreciate the pep talk, but you're forgetting the part where I'd have to be my own salesperson." Her nose wrinkled at the thought. *Nightmare.* "Besides, if I lost all of Rob's money, I'd never be able to forgive myself."

"Sometimes you need to take a risk," Tara said.

"I think a job interview is enough risk for one day."

"All right, I'll back off. I have to run to a meeting, but good luck today. Call me when you're done."

"Thanks, I will."

Jenna hung up, and walked over to the gilt-edged mirror in the foyer, smoothing the collar on her blue button-down shirt as she looked at her reflection. In the silk top and crisp slacks she exuded power and confidence. Still, she'd rather be wearing jeans and a sweatshirt. If she ever got up the nerve to work for herself, she'd be able to spend the day in her drawstring cotton pants and the fuzzy purple slippers that Rob had bought her for Christmas.

Maybe one day. For now, she'd settle for a new job. If she nailed this interview, today could rank up there with getting her driver's license, college graduation, and her first kiss.

At ten o'clock, she went through her red leather tote bag—a splurge in her campaign to break out of her too-sensible tan and black rut—one last time. Resumé. Cell phone. Wallet. Everything was in place, ready to go. Just as it had been last night. And an hour ago. And ten minutes ago.

She didn't need to leave for another fifteen minutes, but she'd rather arrive early and sit in the parking lot than be stressed out over traffic. She picked up a book and tucked it into her bag. Keys in hand, she checked her reflection in the mirror one more time, smoothing the blonde waves that had come loose from her hair clip.

Sliding the tote over her shoulder, she reached for the front door just as her cell phone rang. Shoot. It was the number of the phone Rob used to call her from Afghanistan. Reluctant to miss the call, she shut the door and answered.

Mick's smooth voice greeted her from the other side of the world, and her stomach dipped.

"Hey, I'd love to talk," she said, "but I'm leaving for my interview. Will you be around in a few hours?"

"Jenna, this can't wait."

His use of her given name stopped her dead. He'd been calling her Jay for as long as she could remember. "What's wrong?" She and Mick never discussed anything important. The only thing they had in common was—

A sick feeling settled in her chest and she took a step back, as if she could put distance between herself and what he was going to say. "No."

"I'm sorry," he said, his voice rough and scratchy on the long distance line. "Rob's..." Mick cleared his throat. "He's gone."

Her body went cold. "Gone?"

"We got into a firefight while on a convoy this morning, and Rob was hit." He hesitated. "He died at the scene."

Her throat tightened and she let out a strangled sound of grief.

Mick blew out a long, shaky breath. "I'm so sorry, honey. I wish I could be there right now, but it's going to take me a couple of days to get back. Someone from Claymore will be coming to see you, but I didn't want you to hear the news from a stranger."

"Thank you," she managed, her voice barely a whisper.

Mick urged her to call Tara for support and signed off. Jenna stared at the phone in her hand without really seeing it.

He died at the scene. The words swirled through her brain and brought her whole world crashing down. "No, no, no." Little black spots danced in front of her eyes, and her stomach threatened to return her breakfast.

Rob was done with private security. No more Afghanistan. He was coming home in two weeks. He *couldn't* be dead.

Her legs must have given out because suddenly she was on her hands and knees, staring at the wood floor. "Not Rob, too," she said on a sob, pressing her forehead into the hard, cold surface. It wasn't fair. She'd lost too much already. And now her brother, her protector, her only remaining family, was gone.

Irreversibly, irrevocably gone.

In the biggest picture on the mantle, her family of five was laughing on the beach during a Christmas trip to Hilton Head thirteen years ago. She'd been twelve, Jimmy ten, and Rob seventeen. Now she was the only one left. A reckless driver had seen to that. Her parents had died instantly, but Jimmy had hung on in a coma for six months before finally letting go. Rob had been fresh out of the Air Force with plans to go to school, but Jimmy's medical bills were staggering. So Rob had gone to work for Claymore instead.

Tears splashed onto the shiny wood between her hands, beading up on the buffed surface. If it were possible for a person's heart to burst from too much grief, she'd be joining Rob any second. She wanted to curl into a ball and hide in the dark where she could cry her guts out.

Instead, she stayed glued to the floor until her legs went numb and she was out of tears.

God, she had to get a grip. With a deep breath, she wiped her eyes and stood on shaky legs. Her knees were sore, her toes tingling. She leaned against the front door and snatched up her tote bag from the floor where she must have dropped it. *The interview.*

Somehow she managed to hold it together long enough to call Travers & West. The secretary clucked in sympathy at her reason for canceling, but explained that she couldn't reschedule. They had plenty of applicants and would probably fill the job tomorrow. Jenna didn't have the energy to push the issue.

She slammed the phone down on the kitchen counter and stumbled down the stairs to her one-car garage. The tiny space was stacked to the rafters with boxes labeled in neat print. Soon Rob's things would join them, and her entire family would be reduced to belongings packed lovingly into cardboard. Some people went to a cemetery to commune with their lost loved ones. Jenna hung out in her garage with the boxes. Maybe she was crazy, but it helped.

"It's too much!" she shouted into the whitewashed room as tears threatened again.

Had she wronged someone in a past life? Done something heinous as a child that she'd blocked out? Maybe the Ryan family had picked up a curse somewhere along the way. She laughed—an unbalanced sound—and smoothed her hand across a box of travel souvenirs.

Jimmy's Swiss Army knife from Lucerne, a set of blue and white Delft plates from Holland, an obi—a Japanese kimono sash—her mother had picked up in Tokyo. Bits and pieces of the Ryans' short lives, wrapped in paper and taped up because while she had no place for all the things left behind, she couldn't bear to let them go.

She wiped her eyes and slumped against the wall. She'd give anything to have Rob walk through that door with a hundred-watt smile and lift her into a bear hug. In fact, a hug would be really great right about now.

Tara would be there in an instant if she called, no question, but Jenna wasn't ready to share her pain yet. Instead, she sat there among her boxes until her joints turned stiff.

Finally, she stood and dusted herself off before turning out the lights, and slowly made her way back upstairs. She'd call her friend later. Right now, there was only one thing that could make her feel better. She changed back into her workout clothes and set off for a nearby trail.

Maybe if she ran hard enough, she could outrun the pain.

"WHAT DID YOU find?" Ghost asked the imbecile on the other end of the line as he stared through the floor-to-ceiling window at the sun setting over the Potomac River.

"Nothing more than the documents I took off Ryan's body. Fury got to his things before I could."

"And you're sure Ryan had more evidence?" He squeezed the phone until it dug sharply into his palm. Between these idiots and the asshole who'd discovered them, everything was at risk. The contracts, the money, the company. *Everything.*

"Yes, sir," Beavis said. "Rizzo saw him taking pictures."

"*Fuck.*" He had just over a week to clean up this mess or everything that he'd worked so hard to accomplish would crumble between his fingers like a clod of dirt.

"I thought we might be able to get to his bag on the plane back to the States, but Fury kept it with him, and there were too many people around."

Ghost sucked in a deep breath. A good leader didn't lose his cool. "There's too much at stake for this to get out." He rubbed his forehead. *Goddammit.* None of this shit was supposed to follow them to the States. "Find any evidence and destroy it before he and the girl figure out what they have."

"Yes, sir."

"And if they get in the way…"

"I'll take care of it, sir."

Ghost slammed his phone on the desk. *You'd damn well better.*

GWEN HERNANDEZ WAS a manufacturing engineer and programmer before she turned to writing romantic suspense. She's also the author of *Scrivener For Dummies* and teaches Scrivener (writing software) to writers all over the world. She loves to travel, read, jog, practice Kung Fu, and explore the Boston area where she currently lives with her Air Force husband, two teenage boys, and a remarkably lazy golden retriever. Find her online at gwenhernandez.com.

BOOKS BY GWEN HERNANDEZ

Blind Fury (Men of Steele #1) | Feb 2014
Productivity Tools for Writers | Jun 2013
Scrivener For Dummies | Aug 2012